A MATTER OF TIME

A MATTER OF TIME

LARISSA LOVEJOY

Perspicuous Press

Contents

One

I

Two

II

Three

18

Four

26

Five

34

Six

44

Seven

52

Eight

60

Nine

67

Ten

73

Eleven

81

Twelve

87

Thirteen

97

Fourteen

102

Fifteen

109

Sixteen

116

Seventeen

125

Eighteen

132

Nineteen

139

Twenty

144

Twenty-One

151

First Printing, 2022

ISBN 978-0-6451422-4-2 (pb)
ISBN 978-0-6451422-5-9 (eb)

Cover Image: Cliffs of Moher at Dusk
Credit: elementals, Clément Lelièvre

One

Sonya opened her eyes and found herself lying in a strange bed in a stranger's room. She sat up hastily, shoved her blonde hair out of her eyes, and gazed around the room. A disturbed confusion was written on her face. Where was she? Moving her body, even a small bit, was agony, and she grimaced in pain. As she did so, she saw a man standing behind the doorframe. The curtains in the room were drawn, the light was dusky, and she couldn't see this man properly. What she did see was a large shadow taking most of the door space. She panicked.

"Where am I? Who are you? Ow, why does my head and my leg hurt so badly?"

"Shall I draw the curtains?" The voice was husky and yet musical, in a pleasant, Irish-sounding way.

"Yes, but tell me, where am I? Who are you? Why am I in such pain?"

"Are you hurting terribly?"

"Ow," she grimaced again, "yes, I am, please give me some answers? Where am I? Who are you?" Sonya flopped back on the bed, shaking her head in pain.

The man drew the curtains and sat quietly in a rocking chair in the corner of the room. Unbeknown to Sonya, this man had sat like this almost continually while she'd lain extremely ill in bed. He had revelled in the delight of watching her soft pink cheeks, her blonde hair tied up, and her eyes vivid blue when she occasionally opened them in a daze. Sometimes, she'd tossed the quilt off her shoulders and her abundant shapeliness was clear. This man had his imagination stirred, causing torment. He dropped his eyes to his trusty old Bible that lay in his lap.

Now it was her turn to look. This was her first chance to take in her surroundings. That she was in a woman's room was self-evident. The curtains were pink stripes, there were dainty prints on the walls, and the room had a soft, cosy, feminine feel.

This man's explicit masculinity was a stark contrast. His presence filled the room. There was an unspoken aura surrounding him, but she couldn't bring herself to look directly at him. Curiously, she felt no fear. As she looked out of the window, her eyes squinted at the intensity of light.

"What's out there?"

"Snow, I'm afraid. We're snowed in."

"We? Who are you, and what am I doing here?" Sonya went to climb out of bed, but collapsed onto the pillows, crying out aloud in pain.

The man leapt out of his rocking chair and raced over to her. His look of concern was evident, but it made Sonya feel squeamish. Calmly, he ruffled the pillows behind her, and gently lifted her body so that she was lying more comfortably. She quivered at his touch. It was no ordinary sensation. It combined strength with tenderness, and she was annoyed at being affected by it. She didn't know if he'd seen her quivering. He was very attentive.

"Take another of these tablets. I'm hoping that Seamus can see you soon if they've been able to clear the roads."

"Who's Seamus? Who are you? What am I doing here? How many times must I ask these questions? What's wrong with my leg, and why does my head hurt so much?" She fired these questions quickly and aggressively. Questions tired her.

The man went back to the rocking chair, and said, "sh, go to sleep."

"No, I can't sleep until I know what's happening. What day is it?"

"It's Thursday."

"Thursday?" Sonya lay there trying to remember Wednesday, Tuesday, and Monday for that matter. She tried in vain. As if it might help her to remember, she opened her eyes. She absorbed more of this man who was rocking rhythmically. Sometimes, he stared out of the window at the lightness of the snow, other times, she caught him looking at her. He held her gaze.

The power of his scrutiny made her feel captured. It was a meaningful look between a man and a woman, powerful, hard to interpret, but reminding her starkly of her femininity.

Sonya summarised his appearance. He was tall, she'd seen that when he stood in the doorway. He had a well-proportioned body with broad shoulders, and dark, almost jet-black hair, with a slight wave. He could be a male model, a surf lifesaver, or a bodyguard. His frame was muscular, well-toned, as if he had an occupation that required an impressive-looking, strong body. His face was perfect if that's possible. There wasn't a flaw to be seen, there was nothing she disliked about it. It was a carefully chiselled face.

When he caught her look, she saw deep dark eyes, and as though she was gawking into the depths of his soul, she winced, not only in pain, but for the enraptured tenderness she saw. Her face became flushed, a gentle pink flowing over her cheeks.

Misinterpreting her cry of pain, he hurried over to her again with a painkiller, and thoughtfully soothed her brow. Unkindly, she threw his hand away, not wanting him to know how pleasurable his touch was. Instead, she brusquely demanded, "please tell me, what's your name, and what happened to me? Why am I here and what have I done to my leg?" His attractiveness tugged at her heartstrings and this time she held his gaze. He was silent for as long as she dared to hold his powerful look. She looked away, subdued.

Ignoring her specific questions, he asked the rhetorical question, "you're Sonya, aren't you?"

"How do you know that?"

"Well, you have been in our village now for four months. It's a small enough village for everyone to know each other, and we all know that you're Sonya Painter, the American woman who bought the artist's prize-winning architecturally designed house. We know that you won't take up any invitation anyone gives you; that it doesn't matter if it's the area vicar, the bingo team, or just a friendly neighbour wanting to make you feel welcome. We see that you come out of your house only when you need provisions from the village shops, and that you often walk along the beach, alone, apparently lost in thought, wearing a hat pulled down over your head. We've given you the privacy you seem to want, but it's true, we're curious to know why someone like you wants to hide away."

"You know a lot about me." The gruffness in her attitude was unbecoming. She was astonished at his thorough summary. "Who's the 'we' you refer to, and what do you mean someone like me who wants to hide away? And, as I keep asking, who are you?"

"We're the locals who live within a five-kilometre radius of the village post office, the pub, the church, the local primary school, and the market square, the centre of life for us."

"What does it matter to you all anyway, what I do with my life? Whatever I do is my business, mine alone." She averted her eye from this man, trying to avoid the intensity of his probing look.

"Oh, come on Sonya. You must have known when you bought a cottage on the outskirts of a small, Irish village in County Donegal, that everyone would want to know as much as they possibly can about you. That's the nature of village life from time immemorial. Whether you like it or not, you can't avoid our intimacy, everyone cares about everyone's business."

Reluctantly, she agreed. "I suppose you're right, but I wanted to meet people in my own good time."

"I have to conclude that you think you're not ready for us. Some of us would like to get to know you." He paused to let her absorb this fact. "What are you hiding Sonya, or who are you hiding from?"

Sonya lay there, the medication doing its soothing work, looking at this man. On all her meanderings, she hadn't seen him before. It was rather unnerving that he seemed to know so much about her, when she didn't even recognise his face. She thought she knew all the locals by sight, most of them even by name, not that she'd let on to people about that. It was true, she had come to this village wanting to hide away until she was ready to come out of the protective cocoon that was her lovely little cottage. She'd lived for months now inside the anguish of her throbbing head.

Her attention drifted from herself to this man. While she didn't know him at all, there was something about his manner that made her instinctively trust him. This confidence was strange. She'd spent most of her time these last months trusting no one, living off her wits, feeling desperately lonely in the process. Telling herself that she wanted to be by herself was one thing, admitting that she was screaming out inside with the pain of solitude, was another. How did this man know so much about her when she'd not even seen him before? These human puzzles irritated her.

"Hiding," she muttered, "hiding, hiding, hiding, always hiding."

"What are you hiding Sonya? Who are you hiding from?" He asked these questions kindly, as if he cared about her, not as if he wanted to intrude into the spaces where she wanted no one to venture close to.

As the man stood up, Sonya appreciated how tall he was, she saw him duck easily under an old wooden beam, clearly familiar with its height. His movement was smooth, his body was supple, he glided like a sleek panther. She conceded that he was the most stunning looking man she'd ever seen in real life. He reached the bed and sat on the edge. His nearness unnerved her.

More aggressively than she meant to sound, but as if her belligerence might scare him away, she retorted, "nothing, I'm not hiding from anything or from anyone." Briefly, she glared at him as if he was an enemy rather than someone who, unbeknown to her, had saved her life and helped her these last days. She looked deeply into those beautiful eyes and realised that it was difficult to be nasty to this man. His eyes expressed a profound concern for her welfare. She softened without realising it. "What's your name?"

"Malachy. Malachy O'Sullivan."

"Malachy." The name ran around her head. Why was it racing around as if it didn't want to escape? "Malachy, what am I doing here?"

"Do you really not remember?"

"If I did, I wouldn't be asking, would I?" Irritability crept rapidly into her voice. She wasn't always this crotchety. However, his presence sent shivers down her spine, and these weren't altogether disagreeable sensations. No man had been near her for a long time. She'd kept away from all men. This was no ordinary man. There was a charisma surrounding him, matching his god-like body. Nature had been abundantly generous. Somewhat coquettishly, she twisted a loose tendril.

Malachy twisted his fingers around the curl, and coming near, but not too close, whispered, "this curl is beautiful." With her heart pounding, she pulled back, pushing his hand away, but her hand accidentally brushed his, and the tingle that raced through her body made her shudder in ways that he couldn't interpret, in ways that she didn't want to admit. A man's touch, indeed, the touch of a stranger, warmed something in the core of her being that set her on flame. This was a new experience.

Pretending the tingling touch hadn't happened, she asked again, "Malachy, what happened to me?"

Malachy walked back to the window, turned toward her, looked out at the pure white snow, and then back at her again. A faraway look came into his eyes as if he was remembering details, he wasn't sure he should be repeating. He kept his account factual, hiding his feelings away.

"You were walking on the cliff edge, down at the bottom of my field. The sky was grey. You lay down by the large oak tree and probably fell asleep. In flashes that no one in living memory will remember, a storm arose out of the blue, a storm that had the fury of Mother Nature raging in it. Lightning, thunder, and balls of hail came in quick succession. While I was trying to keep watch of you from a distance, I saw a branch crash onto you."

"How do you know all this?" Sonya asked, curious, flattered to know why he'd been prying. "Why were you keeping a watch on me?"

There was no way he was going to be strictly honest. Instead, he answered, "I was in the garden tidying the rose bushes and saw you walk on the cliff edge. I was concerned that you didn't seem to notice how precarious it is. I was relieved when you stopped by the tree, and I was going to go down to warn you about the dangers of the cliff edge."

"Why would you bother doing that?"

"In this village, we look out for each other. And then the storm came in an unexpected bolt. When the branch crashed down, I knew you were under it somewhere, but I didn't see you move. I was terrified that you were going to roll down the cliff, so I sprinted down the hillside to find you. When I reached you, I realised you weren't going to roll anywhere. A log was trapping you, on your leg and on your forehead. You were unconscious and bleeding. I carried you back to the cottage, dodging hailstones the size of golf balls. I cleaned your gash and tied a piece of sheet around the wound on your head and tried to keep your leg very still. I've attempted to straighten it by tying it to a stick. I'm sorry if it makes you uncomfortable. I then found my sister Fionnuala's nightgown."

"You undressed me?" Sonya asked incredulously and with disgust on her face. Any gratitude to the man who had saved her life was conspicuously absent.

"I had to. It was no big deal."

"You saw me naked?" Anger spread over Sonya's face, distorting her natural beauty. Her body was her body. It wasn't for a stranger to look at, especially while she was unconscious.

"You'll note that you're wearing your underwear. Now I know you might find this hard to believe," and he chuckled to himself, "but I dressed you without seeing your body."

"Impossible! That's impossible!"

"No, it's not. I'm a priest. Under my sweater, I am wearing my priest's clerical collar. I'm trained to be careful in what I do, and I'm particularly used to being discreet in not seeing a woman's naked body."

"You're a priest?" Sonya asked, fear, anger, annoyance, and emotional pain written over her face.

The simple answer came, "yes." Malachy came over to the bed again. Sonya couldn't help but notice his firm, muscular thighs as he stood nearby. She held back her instinct to touch him. This behaviour wasn't like her. "Don't be afraid of me, Sonya." He stroked her hair back away from the material strip that he'd tied around her forehead. Again, she thrust his hand aside, quivering as his warmth raced through her, making her heart pulsate. He lit a fire inside her, a flame not easily quenched.

"A priest!" The comment hovered, ignored except for a slight flicker of amusement across Malachy's striking face.

"Sonya, by the time I'd settled you here in bed, the freak storm had become ferocious. I went to phone my good friend, Dr Seamus Mallory, but the landline phone lines were down. There was no mobile coverage. In fact, they're still down, which is why you remain here. I was deeply worried about you; I didn't know what I was going to do. I couldn't leave you to get help. The snow was deep and had iced over. You were unconscious but restless, tossing to and fro in pain, oblivious to my presence. I gave you whatever painkillers I could find. By the time you were calmer and sleeping, more snow had fallen, and the rest is history. This has been my home from home for thirty-four years, and I've never seen snow pour from the heavens as quickly as it did and build up as high and as solid as it remains. The roads were unpassable. All I could do was wait, pray, and watch over you."

Little did Sonya know how conscientiously he'd watched over her. Malachy had sat observing Sonya closely, the woman who he'd watched often, from afar. Her haunting loneliness and desire for solitude used to upset him, not that he'd discussed this with anyone else. He had often stood on the top of the cliff, watching her stomping along the beach below, unaware of anything but her tortured thoughts.

While she lay in bed, he'd enjoyed the opportunity of watching her closely and uninterrupted. Such a beauty in a woman stirred parts of his priestly being that he knew shouldn't be awakened. Her cheeks were clear and soft. He had stroked them to calm her. Her lips were rosy and kissable, and his imagination had wandered. These meanderings were dangerous, and yet he revelled in the unaccustomed thrill. Her hair was the most beautiful hair he'd ever seen. He had touched it, marvelling at its curly loveliness. Yet beauty and pain were tangled in this woman.

Sonya was silent, taking in what she had heard. She was struggling to come to grips with Malachy's story, and more importantly, with Malachy. A priest? It didn't make sense. She hadn't noticed his priestly collar. She had no concept of a Catholic priest being young, handsome, and virile looking. As a Protestant, she had stereotyped priests to be older, almost secretive, furtive men, who were inexperienced with bodies and women, but were present at christenings, weddings, confessions, and burials. At this last thought, distress streaked across Sonya's face as unwelcome memories that she'd tried to thrust aside were resurrected.

Malachy missed nothing. "What is it, Sonya? What thoughts come to haunt you and cause you such anguish?"

His perceptiveness intimidated her. "What does it matter to you?" She instantly hated herself for being unkindly defiant because she knew that he was being astonishingly attentive to her needs. She asked, "why have you bothered so much with me, caring for me and fussing over me these last days?" Sonya knew that she must sound ungrateful, harsh, and heartless. At this moment, she didn't care.

Malachy turned away to disguise his real feelings. It was far too soon to admit anything to the beautiful, pained woman lying on his dear sister's bed. It wasn't too soon to admit his intense feelings to himself, but as a priest, the enormity and gravity of these feelings were overwhelming. He suspected the exact reason why he cared for her. But in a lighter tone than he had meant, he answered casually, "I'd have done it for anyone."

Curiously, Sonya appeared disappointed with this answer. He had treated her as if she was someone very special. "Can you help me out of bed please? I need to use the bathroom." She then wondered how she'd used it earlier. Embarrassed, she didn't ask.

Malachy watched as Sonya tried to move, could not, kept trying, and in frustration, fell back again, her head shaking on the pillow from one side to the next. "I'll carry you. In case you're wondering, I've done so several times already. You were semi-conscious, aware enough to manage. Put your arms around my neck," he said offhandedly as if the physical contact was no big deal. The trouble is, it had been so long since Sonya had been close to another person, let alone have her arms around a man's neck, that she was uncomfortable with this intimacy. She was mortified to think that he'd carried her to the bathroom before.

Sensing, but deftly avoiding her unease, Malachy lifted her into his arms, pulled her nightgown over her knees, and stood briefly, feeling her soft breath on his neck. He was a strong man. For Malachy, it was a delightful, comforting experience to have this woman in his arms.

He moved slowly, savouring her bodily warmth whilst it was possible, keeping her injured leg straight. Sonya was fighting mixed emotions. The fact that this man was a priest was an enigma. The fact that he was completely gorgeous and utterly desirable, and totally unselfconscious about his appeal, irritated her. She was being irrational. Her thoughts raced to all the good-looking men she'd known in her time and realised that this man was in a league of his own.

Absolutely nobody matched up to this man. He was a priest. She shouldn't be alone with him.

Two

Malachy waited for Sonya, then took her to a different room, lay her on a sofa, pulled a quilt over her, and disappeared. Sonya absorbed her new surroundings, a comfortable, simple Irish cottage. It was decorated traditionally with white stone walls. It had picturesque windows trimmed with neat curtains, lots of dried flowers on the windowsill, and an open peat fire was burning.

Malachy reappeared with a tray of warm soup and bread. "You've not eaten for days."

Sonya ate slowly, pretending not to notice that Malachy's eyes rarely left her. He seemed totally preoccupied, and she found it hard to believe that he was merely a kind priest trying to help an injured neighbour. She saw the intense look in his eyes. As a woman of the world, who unlike this man, had dated, fondled, and made love, she'd seen that look in many men's eyes before, and shyly, she deflected her gaze. But there was something powerfully attractive about his eyes. As soon as she caught his glance for even a flicker, their eyes refused to separate. Magnets were supposed to come together. They weren't. He was a priest. This was a forbidden attraction.

For Sonya, avoiding the need to be with others was the whole point of finding this lovely little remote village off the west coast of Ireland, with a perfect artist's cottage for sale. She'd seen it advertised on the internet, talked to the real estate agent, and struggling to understand his accent, she travelled to check it out. It was perfect. The sale was quick, and her goods arrived speedily.

The cottage was her retreat from the ugly memories of the past, recollections that were painful, recurring in their terrifying guise. To change the topic in her mind, she looked out of the window at the snow, a sight that was breathtakingly beautiful. Avoiding Malachy's eyes, she enquired formally, "tell me about yourself. Why is this place a home from home? Where is your sister?"

Malachy's dark soulful eyes shone. He clearly knew love of some depth. At the mere mention of his sister, affection lit his face. "Fionnuala and I were orphaned at a young age. I was fourteen, she was ten. The local village people were kind to us. They fed us, and while we slept at the stern schoolmaster's house during the week, we were relieved to return to this beautiful cottage every weekend. This is our family home. Fionnuala and I are devoted to each other."

"So, what happened when you went into the priesthood?"

"Aye, that was different, things inevitably changed. I went into the seminary straight after school. An aunt took Fionnuala in until she went off to university to study international relations and journalism. She's a bright spark. Whenever we could, we'd arrange to meet back here. This place is a refuge. It's somewhere we fall back on when we need comfort or love, or when we don't know what we need, but we're searching for something."

This confession was too personal for Sonya. She flinched and tightened up, clenching her hands under the quilt. She wished that he was an old man with wrinkled skin and a shrivelled torso, not a man with an impressive body that would make any bodyguard proud. Memories of his body close to hers as he'd moved her back onto the pillows, and then later lifted her onto the sofa, were fresh. The effect of such seemingly trivial touch was enormous on her sense-deprived body. No one touched her these days, not even a handshake had crossed her palm for months. This man was tantalisingly attractive. She'd come to this quaint Irish village to avoid men.

Trying to change the direction of her thoughts, she asked, "so what are you searching for?"

His reply sent her reeling. It shot out unexpected, like the bolts of lightning that had knocked the branches off the tree and onto her leg and forehead, she felt struck. "Love."

"Love?" she asked, disbelief sprawled over her face.

"Yes, even some priests search for love."

"Intimate love?" Sonya asked automatically, then regretted her hastiness, for this man kept on unhassled, tempting her into personal, secret territory where she had travelled many times before, and now, was trying to avoid.

"Yes," Malachy said, with force, "intimate love. Sonya, I want you to forget that I'm a priest, you'll be able to cope with me better."

"That's a bit ridiculous, isn't it? I'm not sure why you think I'd want to cope with you anyway." Her anger hung from the rafters, heavy and dark. "Besides, if I'm to forget you're a priest, do you want to forget that I'm a woman?"

Malachy's easy laughter filled the room, a warm, engaging, masculine laugh that she wanted to sit back and enjoy forever, but she pretended that the joyous chuckle hadn't affected her acutely. Abruptly, he stopped laughing. His mood changed. He was suddenly serious, and with passion he said, "Sonya, I could never forget you're a woman."

All Sonya could think of was handsome Malachy undressing her, then dressing her in his sister's nightgown, and wondered if it was possible to do this without seeing her body. Her body was well-toned, maintained by exercise and yoga. She knew that men liked to look at her feminine shapes and curves. That he was a man as well as a priest was conspicuous. She wished he wasn't so charming. How much had he looked at her? Again, she changed the subject. "How can you, a priest, be searching for love?"

"That's what I meant when I said you should forget about me being a priest." He stood up and paced about, seemingly anxious, as if he needed private space.

Sonya could relate to this, so she let him be, relieved for the quiet. At this stage in her life, she couldn't contend comfortably with personal revelations. She realised how out of touch with other people's lives she'd become. Her own needs were great; she couldn't listen to others' tales.

"Don't worry," she said, "you don't have to explain anything." She wasn't being merely polite. She meant it.

"Oh, but you don't understand, I want to explain myself." His tone said a lot, and Sonya looked away, abashed. Malachy sat on a stool beside the sofa. Sonya had forgotten what human familiarity was like, how it could unnerve and excite, how one could simultaneously desire and be repulsed by such sparks. On one level, she wanted this attention, on another level, it frightened her.

"Malachy, forget it, please." She was uptight. Seeing him this close, everything about his facial features were perfect looking. She hadn't dreamt it. He had clear, closely shaven skin, a firm chin with a hint of a dimple, strong white teeth, luxuriously wavy jet hair with not a wisp of grey, and those eyes, they kept drawing her into pools of intimacy that she was terrified of plunging into. She feared drowning.

"I can't forget it; I want to tell you."

"Perhaps I don't want to hear."

"I don't want to be inconsiderate to your wishes, but you are part of my story."

"Malachy, don't!" This was a demand. Sonya was frightened. She was being silly. Malachy had only been kind, gentle, caring, and dare she admit it, loving, but whatever he wanted to say to her, she wasn't ready to hear it. Her feminine intuitions told her that his story did involve her. She'd read the messages in his eyes, and felt his body mould warmly to hers, desirous, though forbidden. This man wasn't someone to be put off easily. He was as steadily persistent as she was obstinately reluctant. His gentle forcefulness was part of what made him so attractive. He stroked her forehead lightly, trying to ease her tension, but his touch startled her, and she would not be comforted.

"Sonya, it's okay. Let me explain myself."

"You're a priest, go away."

"I doubt it would be any different if I wasn't a priest, that's what I was trying to explain. I read intense pain in your eyes, a hurt that goes deeper than your leg and head. Talk to me. Let me help you."

"No." With this declaration, Sonya turned away, wincing with physical pain. "I can't concentrate. My leg is very sore. Is it broken?" She whimpered, the pain had become excruciating.

"Yes, I'm sure it is. I suspect the doctor will get through today. I went outside to assess the roads while your soup was heating. The roads are clearer, and Seamus has a snowplough on his car. The village raised money to ensure that he had this provision. He drops in after any drama like the last few days to see if I know of anyone who needs help. He's a good man, he'll assist you."

"Thank you," she replied, knowing she was in urgent need of medical treatment. Extreme pain had returned, cutting through her right leg if she moved it even a slight bit.

Malachy was sitting on a cushioned stool beside her, not within reach. The distance made it easier for Sonya to manage his presence. Malachy might be a priest, but clearly, he was experienced at judging a woman's reactions, and she was vulnerable. He tried again. "Can I tell you my story Sonya?"

Needing something to take her mind of her pain, she responded, "if you want."

Ignoring her cool reaction, Malachy began. "I'm on a unique leave from the priesthood. The church has been part of my identity all my life. It's my family, the centre of my world, and the reason to get up in the morning, and go to bed at night. My entire meaning for life revolves around the church. For some years now, I've been fighting a void, an absence in my life. When I became a priest, I took the vow of celibacy. My commitment to the church was absolute, there was nothing that could stand in its way. I managed this vow easily through my late teenage years and through my twenties. But for these last four years, I'm making more trips back to my cottage, trying to connect with my sister, Fionnuala."

"Have you?"

"Have I what?"

"Connected with Fionnuala?"

"Oh yes, our relationship is delightfully rich. She arrives home shortly. She's been doing some political journalism in Argentina and is due home for some leave." For a while Malachy was quiet, a pensive look on his handsome face. He rearranged his stool closer, looked at Sonya's anxious face, and shuffled back to his original position.

"Go on." Sonya was disturbed by this cordial companionship, and his body near to her own, but she was curiously fascinated by the story.

"My frequent trips home are an excuse for my deep need to connect with that which is most intimate. For four years now, I've been tormented with the idea that my first bond in life is to the church, and my second bond is to my sister, but that I will never know..." He broke up, unsure of how to complete the sentence.

"Will never know what?"

With a deep breath, he answered. "I'll never know the deep love of a man to a woman, a woman who is not a sister, but is his lover, dearest friend, and beloved wife. My superior at the seminary is a wise man, dear Father Paddy Ryan. We've talked about everything over the years, and he's known me all my life. He's my father-figure, father-confessor, and trusted confidant. He's given me time off work to determine my priorities. You see I wanted to work out whether it's intimacy that I really wanted more than anything else before I fell in love, but..."

Uncharacteristically, he stopped in flow. Their eyes met and held, albeit fleetingly, but in a way that communicated some bond, however tentative.

"Go on."

With a change of humour, he said, "but what? But that's life." And he sprang into action on hearing the distant sound of a snowplough chugging its way through piles of snow. "Rescue is on the way, my dear." The endearment tripped lightly off his tongue, sounding natural, not out of place.

Sonya shuddered in mixed emotions. Her mind was a whirlpool. The activities of the last days that had laid dormant in her while her aching body had slept, raced around taunting, confusing, and most definitely, tempting her. It was easier to submit to the pain in her leg and in her throbbing head then to try to make sense of the thoughts in her mind, and the emotions that were bamboozling her.

"There's a damsel in distress I hear, you poor dear. At least you've had Father O'Sullivan to care for you. What a mercy he found you, thank God for that. The snow piled up so quickly that you might never have been found until too late. Oh, my God, I shouldn't be talking like that. Hello, my dear, I'm Dr Seamus Mallory, your local doctor. So, I get to meet the oh so lovely American woman that's moved into our corner of the woods, do I? Not that there are many trees here, so why am I talking about woods?" He took a break in his quick patter to chuckle. "How are you? Now let's look at this leg of yours. Oh, that's a nasty break if I've ever seen one. You must be in unbearable pain. Come my dear, I'm on my way to the hospital, I'll take you straight away."

"Thanks Seamus." The look of relief on Malachy's face was obvious.

Seamus fussed around her in a kindly, reassuring, confident manner that put her at ease. It was easy to like this outgoing bear of a man. "Come Malachy, I want to keep the legs as still as possible. I'll carry these legs, and you lift Sonya's body."

Again, Sonya found herself nestled into the warm chest of this priest-man who she found impossibly charming. In pain with the movement of her leg, she allowed herself to enjoy the bodily contact with this adorable man. Shutting her eyes, she avoided the intensity with which she knew he was looking at her. She lay back in Seamus's car with her eyes shut, listening to muffled voices.

The last thing she heard was a musical voice saying something about looking after a precious bundle. She grimaced as a stab of pain rippled up her leg.

Three

The next time Sonya woke, she gazed around her, confused. Again, she was in a strange place. There seemed to be peculiar things happening continually to her these days. Everything around her was hospital white. The pain racing down her right leg was excruciating. This leg lay uncomfortably in traction, nestled in a cold iron pulley, stuck straight out in an awkward position. Her hand went up to her head. Something felt wrong. A tight bandage wound itself around her entire head. Her hand reached frantically to touch her hair, but she couldn't find it. She became anxious and fretful.

A nurse came in at that moment, jolly, noisy, unflappable. "Hello, what's wrong?"

"Where's my hair? What's happening?" Sonya burst out crying, confused, distraught, and in pain.

"Sh, your hair is fine. It's been tied back out of the way of the bandage, and only one curl from your lovely head has been lost. You had a cut that needed stitching on the front side of your hairline. Don't worry, your hair will cover it, there won't be an obvious scar. You had a terrible break of the leg, and no thanks to the nightmare of the storm we endured, your leg had set wrongly in place because of the time lapse. It had to be rebroken and reset. You'll be in traction for a few days, plaster for six weeks, but physiotherapy will help to get the leg moving again and keep your good leg strong. You've got a long haul ahead of you. Dr Mallory signed your consent to surgery forms as we weren't sure who to contact on your behalf. Now you're awake, who would you like us to contact? You need visitors to cheer you up. Where's your family?"

The nurse paused waiting for an answer. Impatiently, Sonya retorted, "let me be. I'd rather be alone."

Ignoring this reaction, the nurse persevered, "where's your family Sonya? America is a long way away, but you live here now, perhaps there are friends you'd like us to contact."

"Nobody. Do you hear me? I want nobody. Leave me alone. I'll be alright. I need some painkillers. Then, leave me in peace to allow my leg to get better. I just want to go home by myself."

"People get better when they have dear ones to cheer them up. I'm just trying to help you." The nurse's voice was soft, a musical Irish lilt soothing and calming.

But Sonya would not be calmed. "Leave me alone. Stop fussing. I'll be alright."

This sort of conversation went on for days. Regardless of who tried to talk with her, Sonya wouldn't listen, heed, or change the tone of her remarks. Every nurse who tried to get her to soften, left the room disappointed. Unbeknown to her, Sonya was the subject of lively discussion in the nurse's quarters. It didn't seem right to them that a woman as young and as beautiful, despite the bandage on the hair tightly pulled away, could be so cold.

She was hard as a rock. She seemed brutally obstinate. She responded positively to no one. She didn't seem to care who she hurt. That she was hiding enormous inner turmoil was conspicuous to their trained eyes, and to their kind personalities. No one could get her to reveal anything or get her to mellow her tone. This woman was brick hard, insensitively abrupt, and stubbornly unyielding. The combination of physical beauty with emotional hardness seemed unnatural. Many of the nurses turned away, discouraged.

Dr Seamus Mallory, knowing of the nurses' concern, was also worried with Sonya's progress. He agreed that his patients got better rapidly when they were surrounded by loved ones who brought flowers, fruit, chocolates, magazines, music, and most of all, their loving attention.

She was warm enough with him, well, if he had to admit it, she wasn't brusque, but he had busy hospital rounds, there was only a limited amount of time that he could spend with her.

Disturbed by her haunting loneliness, he sent his wife Dymphna to visit her. Dymphna was a big, cuddly, warm, friendly, human being with good intentions. She tried to draw Sonya out, to chat generally about local happenings in the village, and make her smile. Sonya wasn't rude. Indeed, she was civil, but she refused to relax or be responsive. Strong-willed Dymphna left disheartened.

After some time, the bandages came off Sonya's head. That was a relief. The tension on her brow had annoyed her. Instead of letting her hair hang loosely as the nurses had anticipated, she demanded that they tie it back tightly in a topknot on her head, just as she'd done every day when she'd gone into the village or strolled alone on the beach. Pulling her hair starkly off her face seemed symbolic of something, of what exactly, no one could guess. It made her appearance harsher than it should have been.

Sonya had had loads of time to mull over life these last days. They hadn't been easy days. She'd been in a lot of pain. The one person who brought a light to her eyes, that made her smile in her sleep, was the memory of a tall man with broad shoulders, firm muscular thighs, a striking face, and wavy dark hair. The memories of this man were exceptionally pleasurable, reminding her of the small amount of enjoyment in her life these days. She recalled the depths of his eyes, opened her blue eyes, and was startled to see these magnificent alluring dark eyes inches away from her own.

Malachy touched her face gently. The touch was like a soft feather being brushed seductively over her face. She shivered in delight. No one saw this. A nurse stood in the doorway, and noted the spark in Sonya's eyes, saw Father O'Sullivan, crossed herself religiously, and raced off to tell the news that Sonya had woken from the dead, that someone at last had touched a chord in her being.

"Sonya, I brought these for you, I picked them myself." Malachy plopped a luxurious bunch of wildflowers tied with a piece of string into her hands.

She reached for them, and their fingers tangled momentarily as he handed them to her. The touch, although brief and light, had an intense effect. She'd been deprived of sensual stimulation for so long. The feather-soft touch was welcome. Never had such a brief touch induced such an extensive reaction. Her eyes beamed, although her smile was brief. She breathed the perfume of the flowers deeply.

"These are beautiful flowers, thank you." For some peculiar reason, almost as if she was reading his mind, her hand reached instinctively up to her hair that was pulled tightly off her face.

"The curls Sonya, where are those magnificent blonde curls? Why do you hide them away, along with the rest of yourself?"

With that comment, Sonya crashed back to the reality that was the life she lived, the life she hid from, the exquisite pain she kept thrust inside her. Evasively, she answered, "we all hide something away, Malachy."

"Yes, but some hide more than others. You hide a lot."

"Come to torment me, have you?" She didn't mean to be nasty, although she suspected she sounded it. She regretted her tone immediately she'd spoken.

He refused to let her continue in this negative, destructive way. A simple joke about her hair and probing into what she was hiding was enough to scare her. He tried to be light-hearted, but something powerful had closed over.

She was locked into herself. It was like she'd shut the gate that led to her soul, and she wasn't letting anyone in. Occasionally, she'd wander out to the gate to see who was there, act almost as if she was going to open the gate and let a guest in, then, as she glimpsed the person standing there wanting to be let in, fear flowed through her, and she released the vicious guard dogs. They were fierce, nasty brutes, chasing everyone away. She threw them a bone.

Despite this clamming, Malachy chatted effortlessly, his informal approach disguising his concern for her and the desire in him, the craving that as a priest he'd never experienced, the longing that as a priest, he couldn't express. Despite sensing that it was against her best wishes, Sonya refused to respond warmly to Malachy.

Knowing that this time he was a beaten man, that he'd done all he could to bring her out of herself, he left with a sad look creeping over his face. He said goodbye from a distance and stood in the doorway looking back. Their eyes met, refusing to acknowledge honestly what each other was saying. With one last glance over his shoulder, he left.

Nurses rushed back in, hoping to see an animated woman, and instead, were confronted with a mature woman crying, warm tears pouring down her face. They were sympathetic, human beings, as well as professional caring nurses, but she would neither talk nor listen to them.

She continued to snap responses when she had to, then she screamed, "leave me alone. Leave me in peace. Leave me to cry by myself." They did. There was no other option. This woman was severely emotionally distraught.

When she was alone again, Sonya relived the last minutes. She couldn't believe her reactions. The one person she'd been hoping ardently to see again, the one person who made her eyes sparkle, who'd kept her hope alive while she lay in semi-drugged consciousness had visited her. This wonderful man had brought her hand-picked, fragrant wildflowers, showered her with his thoughtful smiles, and she had rejected him. She felt stupid, cross, and totally alone. While he was with her, she felt his presence in the air that she breathed. It was a comfort. His physique and the taboo nature of his body was a high attraction. What you can't have, often you crave. Everything about him heightened her senses and made her conscious of her womanhood. She'd rejected him, and the void left her feeling empty.

Days passed and she tried to make sense of the horrible months behind her. Sometimes, she willed the memories that still tortured her as if she deserved the pain they brought. Other times, she pushed them out of her consciousness, unable to cope with the darkness. Still other times, the memories wafted in and out of her mind. With this drifting, at the merest hint of pleasantry about her past, agonising, negative, and tortuous dimensions overcame the earlier hint. Yet she knew that if she was to come to terms with days gone by, she'd have to deal diligently and thoroughly with these painful memories. She couldn't push them aside for the rest of her life.

Also, she knew that she couldn't shove aside the image of Malachy, who had cared for her, even though she'd rejected him. As quickly as she came to these thoughts, she discarded them. They were ridiculous fantasies. This man couldn't have cared lovingly for her; he was a priest-man. He hardly knew her.

What she couldn't realise was how frequently he had noticed her since she set foot in the village. His observations were from a distance, and more recently, at close quarters while she lay in his sister's bed. Then their stilted conversations from the cottage rushed back to her.

Just as these confused ideas were racing around her brain, causing her to become restless, her mind was nudged to the present by a voice that had that same familiar, refreshing lilt to it, but was a feminine version. She looked up to see a woman standing by her bed. She didn't need any introduction. Anyone with that same black wavy hair, those fine features, that honest looking face, and those remarkable deep dark eyes, had to be Malachy's beloved sister. Furthermore, there was a similar commanding presence about the way she carried herself, tall and remarkably self-confident, yet with no haughty arrogance.

For the first time for days, Sonya showed joy and smiled. "You must be Fionnuala."

"How did you know?"

"You're very like Malachy, aren't you?"

"Only just a bit. I'm wicked, erratic, and impetuous, and I fall in and out of love. He's good, careful, and thoughtful, and falls in but never out of love." The laughter was spontaneous.

"How can he do that? He's a priest."

"Yes, and he's my dear brother, and I adore him to the moon and back."

The women chatted easily as if they'd always known each other, and were just catching up on news, except that the news was novel to them both. Fionnuala told her about her life in the cottage with Malachy, how she was heart-broken with loneliness when he went to the seminary, even though she was proud of him, how the village was never the same without his happy smiling face about the place, and how she used to love to come home from university to be back in the cottage with him again. She talked of some of the adventures of her journalistic career, and the sadness and highlights of visiting trouble spots on the globe.

While she was scared to ask the question, Sonya plucked courage anyway. "And love Fionnuala, what do you mean you've fallen in and out of love?"

Fionnuala readily told her of the men who'd featured recently in her life, James the cameraman in Peru, Jason the fellow journalist in Brazil, Stefan the businessman in Cuba, and Petro, an Argentinian poet who she'd recently broken off with. "And I always rush back to my darling brother."

Her eyes met Sonya's eyes, as penetrating as her brother's eyes. In that meeting, Fionnuala tried to communicate something profound. Sonya was inquisitive but dare not ask questions. She wondered what Malachy had said to this wonderful woman about herself, then wondered why she cared anyway. She did care, why, she knew not.

Every day for five days, Fionnuala visited Sonya. Gradually, everyone in the hospital saw the barricades that had locked Sonya's heart in, tumble down, ever so slowly, brick by brick, repressed fear by dissolved fear. Fionnuala was artful in the ways of the heart, she knew not to push Sonya too hard. Indeed, she didn't even ask any direct questions, but let Sonya slowly open, and talk only if, and when, she wanted to. Her journalistic skills had taught her much about the art of diplomacy and drawing stories out.

While progress was being made in the communication stakes, Sonya only told her little snatches of information about herself that most of the villagers knew already. Nevertheless, Fionnuala was grateful that Sonya was smiling and laughing more. The worry lines around her eyes, face, and forehead were lessening, and she didn't physically tighten up as frequently as she used to do.

Fionnuala left the hospital wondering about the pain in Sonya's life and how best to help her. She had a very good heart for helping others to heal. She was like her brother.

Four

Sonya looked forward to the visits now, expecting Fionnuala at about the same time of day, so it was with enormous shock that one day, she heard heavier footsteps than usual, and turning, saw Malachy stride confidently into her room. It was a private room, a fact she'd been relieved that she could afford. At this moment, she was particularly glad that she had a room to herself. She wouldn't have wanted anyone to see the dark pink shade spreading rapidly over her face. Whether Malachy noticed this blushing or not, he didn't let on. There was something very decisive on his manly face today, as if he was there on a mission.

"Hello Malachy," she said shyly. "What's behind your back?"

"Two red roses," he laughed and produced the blooms, wrapped in kitchen tin foil. "Straight from my garden, one for you and one for me." He chuckled that wonderful melodious chortle that enticed her to join in. Today, she did, albeit briefly.

"Thank you, Malachy," she said affectionately, as if the mere mention of his name induced a soothing, softening quality that flowed through her very being. He didn't realise how often she'd fallen asleep reciting his name repeatedly. "Malachy, Malachy, Malachy."

"Fionnuala tells me that you've become great friends. I'm glad, but I started to get jealous. She says you're coming out of hospital in a few days' time, so I wanted to come and see you before you leave. I've wanted to come for days, but Fionnuala insisted on coming alone." He was trying to disguise how much he had longed to come. Sonya sensed this and was deliciously flattered. Malachy picked up on her vibes and she hugged this happiness to herself.

"Yes, she's a fabulous person, I like her very much." Coyly looking at him, looking away, and coming back to those wonderful eyes, she looked fully at him again. "I'm very glad you've come to see me today, Malachy. I was rude to you last time and I regretted that. I want to say also how grateful I am to you for taking care of me. You saved my life. Seamus tells me I would have frozen out there in my concussed state, lying under the tree branch. Thank you for helping me."

"It was my pleasure, Sonya," and with a hasty look at the door, he lifted her hand, and naughtily let his lips brush quickly over Sonya's manicured tips. Despite the lightness of the touch, and the soft moistness of his lips, Sonya glowed inside. He dropped her hand suddenly as he walked swiftly and with purpose to the door and shut it quietly. "I may as well make the most of my reputation as a priest while I still am one. A priest behind a closed door is a trusted man." He grimaced a trifle uncomfortably.

"Malachy, what are you talking about?" Sonya looked troubled by his action. An open door signalled openness to the world, wasn't that enough?

"It's all right, my dear," and he reached impetuously for her hand again, then with regret looked toward the door and dropped it gently back onto the bed as if someone was about to burst in and catch them acting inappropriately. "Sonya?" His eyes appealed to her in the most heart-warming manner that she found irresistible.

She sensed that whatever was to come now was to change her life forever. It was hard to explain, but this precise moment seemed of enormous significance. It was impossible to articulate how she knew it, but she sensed that Malachy's face, his demeanour, sounded bells that chimed with precise intent. The noise chimed in her head. This was a moment to savour. Sonya felt shivers of thrilling excitement pass through her body, and flutters of fear of the unknown travelled down her spine. "What is it, Malachy?"

"Sonya, please listen to me." He leaned close to her face as if he wanted to kiss her, then bent away, and sat somewhat stiffly, taking up the proper position of a man of the church. "Do you remember back in the cottage when I was telling you that I was on leave from the seminary?" He didn't wait for an answer, but sped on, urgent with his words. As she'd thought, he was a man with a mission. His purposeful attitude made him seem rugged, and she liked it. "I needed to decide if it was intimacy with a woman that I wanted more than my vocation in the church, and I wanted to decide this before the possibility of falling in love. Well, on the third day of my leave, as I stroked your hair, your beautiful curly hair that for some God-forsaken reason, you pull away for no one to see..." He stopped mid-sentence as they smiled, and Malachy pulled a tiny wisp of curl that had escaped and twirled down her forehead.

"Keep going Malachy." Sonya's voice was breathless with anticipation.

"On the third day of my leave, I felt that maybe I was beginning to understand what it might be like to be in love."

"In love?" Incredulity stuck in Sonya's throat. This declaration wasn't what she was expecting. It wasn't what she wanted to hear. She sucked breath in as she knew her body was tightening in nervous tension.

"Yes, Sonya."

"That's not possible." Her voice was tight, creaky with emotion.

"Oh yes, it is. Listen to me carefully, Sonya, I am leaving the priesthood to explore what love for a woman might mean."

"You can't do that Malachy, not for me. If you wanted to take your leave to think about such a big decision before you fell in love, you're too impetuous to say that you have some understanding of love now. You're probably in love with the idea of being in love. The idea is a lovely concept. But the idea of love, isn't the same as being in love. Love isn't straightforward, it can be messy."

"Nice try, but I have a quiet assurance from God that I am making the right decision. I don't know you yet, but that's part of the amazing excitement I'm experiencing. My life in the priesthood has been a rich time, a valuable journey for me and the people I've helped, but I now look forward to forging a new life, with a woman beside me."

This was more than Sonya had bargained for. She'd sensed that what Malachy had to say would be significant, but not this enormous. This was massive, too big to absorb. "I can't cope with this. I've had more intense emotions than I can handle in my own life these last months and can't handle this intensity."

"I'll not rush you, but I think it would be helpful for you to tell me a bit about yourself. I want to know about the real you, and I can't do this until you communicate more. I suspect you know about love, and perhaps the pain as well as the joys of love. Am I right?" He sensed she was grappling with something enormous inside her, so he ambled away to give her some personal space. He'd observed her vulnerability to the contrasts between closeness and distance, between touching and pushing human contact away.

He watched her from a distance, and as if a gigantic bubble that had been trapping her had risen inside her, and come flowing through and burst triumphantly, she held out her arms to him, waited for him to rush to her, leaned on his firm strong chest, and with her arms clinging around his neck, she sobbed into his dependable neck. These were intense sobs, the outcome of a long, deeply felt pain. Her tears wet his neck, and he clung on.

Risk was not a normal part of his life. What he was doing was high-risk. He tried to move her away as he heard a noise outside the door, but she clung on. He couldn't shove her aside, back onto her emotional scrapheap. But he had to be careful. How would it appear if anyone should walk in? What would anyone think if they found him, the respected and much-loved village priest home from the seminary, where he taught young priests to resist the sins of the flesh, in a tight embrace with a beautiful, clinging woman? He was not a scandal seeker.

"Oh, Malachy."

"Yes, darling."

"You can't call me that."

With a cheeky smile, he cocked his face to one side, and cheekily repeated, "yes, I can, it's used very casually here, from the post mistress to the barman, they call anyone darling."

Sonya's mood changed. She was suddenly sombre. "I want to tell you, my story. I've told no one else since I moved here."

The gravity of this sudden exposure wasn't lost on Malachy. He had not expected it to come for a while. "I'm waiting." He sat back, priest-man again.

"I came to Ireland from California on a holiday. I had just come out of a terrible affair with a selfish married man who hurt me bitterly, and I came to Ireland to escape. My grandparents are Irish and always talked so fondly of the place that I felt as if I knew it already. They described the beautiful scenery, the green fields, the Celtic music, and the friendly people, so I came in search of the solace I thought the place might offer me. I'd trained in California as an artist, and while I enjoy painting, teaching is my first love."

"How interesting."

"Surprisingly, I found a job teaching in an art college in Belfast. I fell in love with the senior lecturer there, an older man called Malcolm who wasted no time in proposing to me. We married, had a beautiful daughter called Katie and a lively, witty son called Matthew. We had six glorious years of bliss together. We were very happy. If there is a heaven, I've had a glimpse of it." She managed to tell this factual part of the tale quickly, but now could go no further, tears filling her eyes.

"I thought you'd known deep love Sonya, please go on." Malachy searched her face for signs of who she really was, not only who she appeared to be.

With a quiet voice, she said, "Malcolm, Katie, and Matt were killed in a car accident. It should have been me, not Malcolm."

"No, my darling, oh, I am so sorry to hear that, it's terrible, absolutely devastating news."

"Malcolm was picking up the children from a friend's birthday party. I was supposed to collect them, but I had a headache, so Malcolm went. The accident was the fault of a drunken driver. If I'd gone to collect the children that day, I'd have been killed instead of my husband. I have never recovered from the loss of my spouse, daughter, and son. I've never understood why my life was spared, yet my entire family's lives were taken. What's the point of that?"

"There are many parts of life like that, moments and happenings we'll never understand. That's the human in me speaking by the way. God's ways are mysterious, often beyond human comprehension, that's me the priest talking."

She ignored his philosophising. "After the accident, I couldn't stay near Belfast anymore. Everything that was familiar reminded me of my hurt. But I didn't want to move back to California either. I can't even keep contact with Malcolm's family. They're the loveliest, dearest family you could imagine, but everything about them reminds me of him, and I can't cope with the reminders. Someday I might be able to, I know that they'd love me to, but not yet. I am just not quite ready."

"One day, you will."

She ignored his sensible comment. "With Malcolm's death, I received some insurance money. I could live simply on this money, so I bought my cottage, hoping to escape from Belfast and my sad memories. I came to this part of Donegal because we took many wonderful family holidays here. The children loved the uncomplicated simplicity of their time away. We loved the peacefulness, the ruggedness, the cliffs, and most of all, the wildness of the ocean. In living here, I felt I could be close to where Malcolm and I found that our soul was refreshed. If I've been rude to people here, I'm sorry. It's taken me a long time to realise that I must live in the real world again. I'm only beginning to do this now by telling you, my story. I've not told it to anyone."

"Oh, my darling, that's a tragic tale. Thank you for sharing it with me."

"Malachy, don't call me that."

"What?" asked Malachy innocently, not having a clue as to what she was referring to. "Don't call you what?"

"Don't call me darling," she whispered.

"It slips out. I used to watch you walk down to get your groceries. I'd be sitting in the village square, home for a day, or a weekend, chatting to the locals, and you were oblivious to me watching you. You were unaware that everyone wants to meet you."

"I can't believe you know details about me when I don't even remember seeing your face around the place."

"You didn't see much of what was going on. Often you walked with your head down facing the ground. You always wore dark, dowdy colours, with your hair tightly pulled back. Why do you never wear it free?"

Quietness hung in the air. It took time for Sonya to answer, and she spoke very slowly. "Katie had loose wild curls like me too. I loved her hair. I tried to plait it and it would loosen itself. Katie always wanted it to be free. Malcolm loved my hair. My instinct was to cut my hair off the day after I buried them. I didn't. I couldn't bring myself to do it, but I wear it tied back deliberately, so that it doesn't remind me of Katie or Malcolm."

"You can't keep hiding Sonya. Under the facade of your dark grimness, I used to see a frustrated youthfulness straining under the tensions. Let go. I don't mean forget, you'll never do that, but don't let the past haunt you so totally, as it obviously has done so far. Grief stays for a long time, with some people forever. But let your new friends help you, Seamus, Dymphna, Fionnuala, and me. Let me remind you of the joys of love again."

"What's the point, Malachy? I've known love and it brought me agonising pain. You've never known love, so you're a novice to its taunts."

"Don't be so sure of that, but that's a story for another day. I'm going to open the door now." To be truthful, Malachy didn't entirely trust himself with the door shut. He was convinced that strange as it was, he was falling in love with this woman who he knew little about. Now that she had exposed some of her painful past, he ached to help her. Not that he was sure of how to do so, or whether she'd accept his offers anyway. At this moment, he wanted nothing more than to hold her close and never let go. She was no more ready for this than the rest of the world was to see their village priest, now in a senior teaching role in the seminary, in love with a woman.

That night, Sonya slept a deep sleep. She was emotionally drained. Her story had been locked inside of her for all these months. Telling the story brought an important release, but she was emotionally exhausted.

It had been a significant exchange of stories. What would the next part of the tale reveal?

Five

Seamus had dropped in to see Sonya regularly, not letting on that he was going beyond the call of duty for a hospital doctor. Sonya welcomed his cheery professionalism. He was a kind-hearted man. While his boyhood mate Malachy had not talked to him fully yet, he sensed that his mate was somehow responsible for the transformation everyone saw in Sonya's demeanour. Seamus suspected that in his own good time, Malachy would talk to him about his heart's desires. He knew Malachy well enough to know that his personal interest with this woman was a momentous decision. He kept this knowledge tucked away, not even sharing it with his chatty wife. Sure, the whole village would know instantly if she knew.

The day before Sonya was due to go home, Fionnuala and Malachy came to visit. It was strange for Sonya to see them together, they were uncannily alike. Sonya felt a little weird with them both there, particularly since she'd shared some of her private life with Malachy, and he'd declared affection for her. She had thought of little else since seeing him. It didn't seem real. How could it be?

The idea of Malachy's declaration of wanting to understand more about love kept revolving around her head, confusing, baffling, but exciting her all at once. She hadn't willed this man into her life. She hadn't been in the social company of men or women for that matter since the accident.

This man was different. He aroused emotions and feelings and sensations in her that she'd never been in touch with before. There was a certain thrill of the unknown. The fact that he was a man that embodied a long, historical, religious taboo disturbed but excited her.

She thought back to her student days. They had been a little wild. Men had courted her, she'd been intimate with many, and slept with some. They were fun days, and she had no regrets about her past relationships. She saw them as part of growing up. Her first and only affair with a married man initially was exciting. He wooed and flirted with her, buying expensive gifts before seducing her. She was a willing object of desire, submissive to his needs. As a wealthy businessman, his lifestyle was vastly different from Sonya's art world. He found the contrast a turn-on. The formal and the informal, the inhibited and the expressive, the world of order and making big money, and the wonders of creative chaos versus painting for fun.

She was indifferent to the contrasts but enjoyed his lavish attention. As she became his mistress, increasingly, he wanted her to jump at his beck and call. He demanded total submission to his every weird desire. Increasingly, he became dominant in their sexual relationship, forcing himself crudely onto her, luring her into acts that frightened and repulsed her. He became nasty as she withdrew and walked away. Refusing to accept her rebuttal, he stalked her, sent her horrible notes, and left pornographic messages on her answering machine. She left California a scared woman, and fled to Ireland, looking for a spiritual retreat.

Malcolm's gentleness came as a welcome relief. Lovemaking was satisfactory, but she wanted to be ravished. She wanted the strength of a man to tousle with her vigorous desires. Malcolm was quiet and tentative. She wondered if she'd lost out a bit because of his lack of liveliness and reticence to experiment. She never let on for fear of hurting him. There were big gaps in her longing.

In Malachy, she recognised the careful tenderness that she loved in a man but suspected that there was a raging virility in his maleness, a potency she'd started to fantasise about. She wondered if he'd had any experience prior to entering the seminary. She'd often dreamt of finding a man who combined compassion with a raging lustiness. No other man had stimulated her imagination as vividly. This was a man who was forbidden to enjoy the fruits of her flesh. Her tastebuds watered at the thought of being a temptress.

Now, Malachy stood before her. She was in little doubt of her joy at seeing him standing beside his sister. Her body came alive in his presence. She was in little doubt of his rapture at seeing her sitting up on the hospital bed. She could sense the restraint in his face, as he folded his arms as if to contain himself. It was like he was holding his physical urges in. Similarly, she knew the constraint in her own body. She longed for his warm arms to fold her in his tight grasp. Instead, her hands lay demurely folded in her lap.

Fionnuala, not insensitive to the electric vibes passing between her brother and her new friend, started joking around to loosen the mood. This didn't help, the couple wouldn't be distracted, and she skipped out of the room. "I'll leave you two to chat over things for a few minutes, then I'll come back." She chuckled to herself, and added, "though I think it's more than a chat that you two need."

"Sonya, my darling," Malachy moved as if to kiss her, but saw her eyes averted to the open door, and turning, saw a nurse pass by. "This is ridiculous, the sooner I leave the priesthood and come out in the open the better," he whispered urgently. His fingers tapped on his thighs, restless, not knowing what to do with his physical energy. The movement on his thighs aroused her imagination, but she was hesitant about the physical stimulation surrounding her. From nothing to an explosion of heightened sensuality, was a drastic change. She wasn't sure if she was ready for it.

"Don't rush into anything Malachy. I've said nothing about my feelings to you yet, and I'm still an emotional mess from the past. You must realise this." She didn't add that she was an emotional mess now, for quite different reasons, her body pulsating with an aching desire. Every sensual stimulus in her was alert. Instead of giving him any clues as to what she was thinking, she reverted to a serious discussion.

"I'm not rushing hastily or naively, but prayerfully, with great con-sideration."

"I get the impression that I entered your life and then you decided to leave the priesthood. Leaving is such a momentous decision to make. I'd hate you to reach a rushed decision that didn't suit you in the long run. Besides, I don't know what I think about you or about anyone else at this moment." This wasn't entirely true. She knew that the mere thought of Malachy's body could incite such delightful images in her brain, that she could hardly contain her emotions or her wild whimsy. His presence stirred in her the precious memories of love, but the awakening unsettled her.

"Sonya, I know you're going to need time to think over any close friendship we might develop, and to make whatever decisions you have to make. That's fine. We both need time. The whole village will be shocked when they find out my decision."

At the thought of how all-encompassing his decision was, she became nervous. The door was open, they were whispering, trying not to look furtive. "Malachy, you can't presume anything. Please don't rush into any decision that you might later regret." Her facial expression was firm. "Have you told Fionnuala yet?"

"Told her what?"

"About my story and your feelings."

"Oh yes, I needed to talk to someone. Apparently, she thought that I was a different man the second she walked through the door. She says I even look different, something about an inner glow," he said in a lower rough voice, wanting her to chuckle with him, surprised that she did not. "I'm not sure how you can have a glow without having done much to bring it on, but I can't keep much from Fionnuala, we've always shared everything." He looked away into the middle distance. "Well, almost everything. I didn't think you would mind if I told her your story. She expressed so much empathy for what you have gone through. My emotions are exploding, and she saw that. I feel like a blind man who's just got his vision. Everything looks completely different when you're exploring love." He saw Sonya wince at this. "Everything to do with love brings back memories, doesn't it?"

She nodded painfully, pushing flashbacks aside, letting new images flow in. "Keep going anyway." Even the sound of his voice was music to her ears, lulling the clanging in her head.

"I'll tell Seamus soon. I think he's guessed bits and pieces already. He's rung me up a few times, fishing for clues, and he's dropped in several times on the way home from hospital for a general chat. He always brings fresh news of you as if I'm expecting to hear about you. I'll tell my other best mate soon. I hope you grow fond of Tim."

"Who's Tim?"

"Tim, Seamus, and I grew up together. We were in the same year at school. Seamus went down to Dublin to medical school, fell in love with Dymphna, and came back to the area he grew up in to be the local doctor. He's a great friend to me, and as you have discovered, he's a wonderful doctor. Everyone adores him. Nothing is too much for him to help someone out. Tim and I went off to the seminary together, but Tim came back as the parish priest, and I went on to do further study, and now I'm a teacher myself in the seminary. Of course, I'm going to have to go back to the seminary soon to tell Paddy my superior what I've decided." He paused.

"And then?"

"And then, in the right time, I may just be able to declare my love for a certain woman and announce it to the rest of the world."

"No, you can't." There was an unpleasant forcefulness in her voice. It didn't suit her. But she wasn't ready to handle the public. Even being so near to Malachy whispering to her was an effort. Talk of the rest of the world literally terrified her.

"What do you mean, no I can't?"

"That would make me look really foolish."

"Why?"

"Because I've not said anything about my feelings towards you, and you can't be sure about me, it's far too quick."

Fionnuala put her head around the door at this moment, took one look at the tense, serious faces, and with gay abandon said, "I'll give you to a few more minutes to work out whatever you're trying to work out, then catch you later." It was impossible not to laugh with her.

Malachy took up the conversation as if there'd been no break. "Okay. I can see that I should go slowly. I am impatient. These new emotions come flooding into me, and I want to deal with them straight away. Tell me that you won't close your mind or your heart to the possibility of finding love again." His voice had such a pleading tone to it, that she couldn't help but feel moved.

Nevertheless, she didn't feel comfortable. "No, I'll not close myself. I had to do what I did in hiding myself away, to come to grips with my sad life and the tragedy that had happened, but I do want to move on. I'm not sure what to move on to, but I want to start to integrate back into normal social living again."

"Good, that makes a lot of sense." Relief flooded his face.

"But I can't promise you anything, Malachy. Please don't assume a single thing. It would be a mistake for you or for me to do or to say anything rash, and it would be unfair of me to you if I was to pretend otherwise. You have to promise to keep quiet about that."

"I've told Fionnuala, and I must tell Seamus, Tim, and Paddy."

"Fine, I can accept that, but swear them all to secrecy."

"Yes, I'll do that, but I am leaving my vocation Sonya, I have decided that already. It is such a major decision, I can assure you, I'm not doing this lightly. I've been pleading with God to give me wisdom." He paused to let the seriousness of his remarks sink in. "And what then?"

"You'll simply have to tell people that you've left."

"I can't. I can't just say that I've left." His face spoke the horror at the mere thought of leaving the villagers dangling, wondering why he'd left the priesthood.

"Why not?"

"Because no one would understand. I'd be disgraced. Here in Ireland, particularly in these close-knit rural communities, being a priest is a revered calling, a real honour. Every parent is proud of their son who has the calling. It comes from God. Every village is proud of the sons that become priests. Now, it'll be hard enough for the locals to accept that I might be falling in love, but accept this they would, eventually, in a matter of time. It won't be easy. I'll receive a lot of criticism and face much anger. Some people won't be able to talk to me or look me in the eyes. There'll be some ostracisation. The older ones will be devastated. In their eyes, I'll have let them down. I'll be a failed priest. I'll have failed the village, failed them. The younger ones will be sympathetic. They want the church to move ahead with the times."

"Given all that, how can you even think of leaving?" She was genuinely worried.

"As I keep saying, I've spent years of my life thinking about this. This is not a rash, reckless move. I want love. But I can't just leave and not be able to give people a proper reason for leaving. That's something I can't do. I owe it to the villagers, people who've been good to me since I was an orphan and have supported me in multiple ways. I must be able to give them a sensible account of my actions."

"Malachy, this is just too much for me. This is something you must work out yourself. It's heavy duty. I'm not ready for it. I don't even know what the 'it' is. I'm not prepared to commit myself to anything. You don't know me. I don't know you. I might end up disliking you. You're forbidden to love. None of this makes sense. Just don't rush into anything. Everything is going ridiculously fast. You must promise me that you won't tell anyone else." She held his gaze. "Do you promise?"

"Yes," he said quietly, and with great reluctance, "I promise."

"Come in Fionnuala," cried Sonya, relieved for the distraction. This time Malachy, left, a forlorn look on his face.

"You okay, petal?"

"Yeah."

"This is new to him, Sonya; understand that. A priest exploring love, the forbidden fruit, wow!" She looked about her, as if the walls could hear.

"I'm not sure that I want this. I don't really know what I want."

"As I'm sure he said to you, go slowly and see what happens. Only trouble is...." She paused, searching for the right words.

"Yes?"

"The only trouble is, I'm not sure he can go slowly. He lives, breathes, and desires the possibility of love with a passion that obviously, he's never known before. I saw the look of ardour on his face the moment I walked inside our front door, as if there was a boiler of energy waiting to explode out of him. Thirty-four years of repression, now wanting a passionate release. Can you imagine the explosion?" She laughed brazenly, but laughed alone, not ashamed of her boldness.

"No more Fionnuala, I'm embarrassed."

"Don't be, but fine, I understand. Before he comes back, I want to talk quickly to you, girlfriend chat."

They whispered together, giggled, and it was with relief that Malachy came back into a room filled with light-hearted murmurs. The three of them finalised domestic arrangements, like the time they would pick Sonya up from hospital and made a shopping list of everything Sonya needed for her larder. They had begged her to come back to their place. She insisted that she was well enough to go home, if someone could fetch groceries. She'd been having intensive physiotherapy to strengthen her good leg as well as the one in plaster, and she was making good progress. Dr Mallory's orders were to exercise appropriately, and to rest sufficiently. She was now skilled with the crutches.

The three chatted easily until it was time to go. Fionnuala did her usual and waved cheerily and left. "See ya tomorrow."

Malachy didn't want to leave. He wanted to embrace her tightly, to show her body how much his body desired her, to show her personhood how much he cared for her. But he was conscious of his public surroundings with busy hospital staff rushing to and fro. He was a priest, simply doing his pastoral rounds of hospital visitation. He grasped her hand briefly, and said, "see you tomorrow." He lowered his masculine, husky voice considerably. "You're coming out tomorrow, and are starting a new life, and I'm part of the newness."

"I'm scared." She was. He saw it on her face and understood it. "Don't rush things, Malachy." She loved saying his name. It was such a sexy name that she wanted to say it again. "Bye, Malachy." They smiled knowingly at each other, smiles that opened new worlds of possibilities.

She sat out in the hospital lounge for the rest of the day, reinvigorating her dormant social skills. Nurses, doctors, and long-stretch patients who'd seen her mope about over these last days, remarked how wonderful she looked. More than once, she heard the whispers, even though those around her tried to be discreet.

"Amazing what successes Father O'Sullivan can work, isn't it now?" commented an old man with a slight grin to his fellow old friend sitting beside him with an equally sly grin.

"Did you see what Father O'Sullivan's chatting to that American woman resulted in? Well, you've never seen such a transformation," said a young girl to her friend, nursing her new-born baby.

"That woman just wouldn't talk to anyone before the priest softened her up a bit," added the young girl's friend.

"I wouldn't mind that Father softening me up a bit," said an older woman who gave her friend a wink and a knowing nudge.

"She'd come in and ask for her groceries and disappear without a word of news," Sonya overheard, not bothering to work out who'd said this.

Back in the solace of her room, she was aware that life after the hospital would never be the same as life before the hospital. She didn't only mean that she had made new friends, and that she'd vowed to break the desperately lonely shell that she'd created around herself. She knew that Father O'Sullivan was a big part of this new life. The local gossipers were right about his influence on her life, if only they knew how accurate.

Within himself, he was already starting to live out the fantasy of life as ordinary Malachy, not life as he'd known it as Father O'Sullivan. It was a complicated scenario, Sonya knew it, Malachy knew it, but whether she welcomed it or not, she was caught in its allure. He transformed her, set her imagination alive, and stirred her sensual passions that had lain suspended for too long.

She waited longingly for the new day and for her new life to begin.

It was symbolic. She knew that waiting for the unknown is exciting, but it is also scary. Changes were happening too quickly. Everything needed to slow down. She would make sure they slowed down.

Six

It was a cold Irish morning, with enough pale blue sky to lift one's spirits. At least it wasn't raining. At last, Sonya was leaving the hospital where she'd gone through cycles of moods, from anger and irritability to a gradual loosening of her troubled soul, and then to a blossoming, a real sense of excited anticipation of what lay ahead of her in the future.

She sat in a chair, waiting for Fionnuala to bring her some clothes. She'd given Fionnuala her house key, money to buy food, and instructions on where she kept her jeans and jumpers. Fionnuala had reminded her that with plaster on her leg, she'd not be able to wear jeans unless she unpicked a seam and she volunteered to do so.

Sonya knew that it would feel strange to be going back to her cottage, and odd to be taking new friends into her private retreat. No one had been invited to visit her in the cottage, and no one had dared venture in uninvited. It was her private sanctuary away from the world of prying eyes, and that was the way she had wanted it, until now.

But what it was that was happening now, she couldn't precisely identify. It had something to do with dealing with her past, it was very much associated with adapting to the present, and the future hovered in uncertainty. Nevertheless, whatever changes she now desired in her life, it wouldn't be easy to have other people in her house, looking at the many objects that reminded her of her past life with Malcolm and the children.

How would she feel with Malachy's eyes fixed on special photos and memorabilia? What were her real feelings toward this man? Was he being rash in his judgements about her? She suspected not. He had taken four years of his life to ponder over his life's priorities, and after prayerfully agonising, he had decided that intimate, sensual love was to be his life mission. Then she felt confused.

What came first, her or his decision? This question was too muddling for words. People didn't fall in love with a widow they knew little about, especially people like Father Malachy O'Sullivan.

She was an intelligent woman, but the problems floating around her brain lead to difficult questions which merged with more questions. What if he left the priesthood and she didn't fall in love with him? That was a highly likely scenario. She didn't know him and wasn't ready for the intimacy he desired. If she spurned his affection, he'd be ashamed, and this might mean not being able to tell the villagers why he'd left the priesthood. That would be too horrible to contemplate. Nothing he'd done made him deserve to be disgraced. But none of these questions were easy to face, and finding adequate answers seemed impossible.

She was brought back to life by the sound of Fionnuala's tinkling voice and laughter that always seem to be present with her. "Where's Malachy?"

Fionnuala chuckled heartily. "Oh, hullo, don't worry about greeting me. I'm a tough cookie. Never you fear Sonya my dear, he's waiting in reception for you to change into these clothes."

"Oh, that's good," Sonya remarked, trying to sound indifferent to his absence. "Hiya, how are you?"

"Nearly thought he wasn't here, didn't you? That must mean something, doesn't it?"

Sonya smiled and nonchalantly shrugged. "Something could be anything, couldn't it?"

"Something is definitely something," Fionnuala quipped.

Sonya pulled on her old familiar clothes with vigour, noting that Fionnuala had thoughtfully and carefully undone the seam of one leg of her jeans to enable her to pull it up over her plaster. She was bursting to get out to see the man who featured so strongly in her vivid fantasies as well as reality.

Two nurses helped her to walk slowly to the reception area. She was now an expert with the crutches. She stifled her natural reactions on seeing Malachy. Her instinct was to hold out her hands and let his arms wrap tightly around her. This was his instinct too. She knew that simply by looking at him. They couldn't do what their bodies' magnets compelled them to do.

With relief, she had a genuine excuse to lean on his strong arms as Fionnuala helped her on one side, and Malachy helped her on the other side. She didn't really need this assistance, as she'd been exercising regularly, building up the strength in her leg muscles so that she didn't have to be overly dependent on others on her return home. But in this instance, as she slowly took a step at a time, she was glad of any excuse to be close to Malachy. Their physical closeness communicated what their hearts and minds were too modest to appreciate.

The mood in the car as the drive home was mixed. Sonya was quiet. Sometimes, Fionnuala and Malachy chatted and bantered about in the easy manner of a brother and sister with a long history of close ties. Other times, Fionnuala sang, her rich melodious voice a pleasure to listen to. She sang Irish folk songs, switching from laments to songs of gay abandon.

Malachy became conscious of how quiet Sonya was. He was watching her in his mirror and saw the pensive look on her face. "You okay, Sonya?" He watched her reflection nod as she looked into the car mirror to catch his eyes. A fleeting smile passed briefly over their faces, although they weren't certain what they were acknowledging.

Malachy drove down her front path. He opened the car door for Sonya, and reached a hand to her, always careful in case anyone was passing by on the street. As his arms helped her out of the car, she knew she was coming home in more than one sense.

It was a thrill for Sonya to be putting her key into her lock again. It had seemed ages since she was home in her sanctuary. "Everything looks very clean and fresh. Thank you."

"Everything is in order, come and see your overflowing larder and fridge. The food should keep you going for some time."

She glanced quickly into the cupboards that Fionnuala was opening, then raced as quickly as her leg would take her to the dining room table. On the table was a bunch of beautiful flowers, a mixed variety of colours of cream, ivory, milk, and snow. These were celebratory flowers.

Out of the corner of her eyes, she caught a glimpse of a card leaning on the vase. She picked it up and read the handwriting. "To my dearest S, in pursuit of love, M." Diplomatically, Fionnuala, who had bought the flowers for Malachy, was nowhere to be seen. Sonya turned and found herself in the powerful arms of Malachy, enfolded by strength and tenderness.

"I'm seeking love Sonya, seek it with me." Malachy whispered his endearment into her hair, which was still caught back tightly on her head. "Oh Sonya, you're beautiful. I want to get to know you fully."

Sonya could say nothing except, "Malachy." How she loved his name! She never tired of saying it. The sound of his name lulled her to sleep, kept her imagination alive in the day, and excited her to repeat it to him in person. She called his name again, saying, "Malachy," as he took her into the folds of his arms. "Thank you for the flowers. They're beautiful. I love to receive flowers."

They spotted Fionnuala at the same time. "I don't want to spoil things for you both, but I have to interrupt you. I don't know how you're going to develop any sort of sensible relationship while you're still a priest Malachy, not just technically, but in real terms." She looked and sounded stern.

"What do you mean in real terms?"

"Sonya, he shares in the church services with Tim when he's home. He's saying the mass this week. He is a priest. You have to accept this fact and be realistic."

"Oh," Sonya remarked innocently, as if the realities of Malachy's situation hadn't fully filtered through to her awareness. How could they have? He held her ardently as an amorous man, not as a priest might hug briefly and nudge one aside, not wanting to risk a scandal.

"Besides, while you can get away with a lot of visitations of the sick Malachy, you can't be seen to be visiting the lovely American woman every day. It wouldn't be proper. And being proper is expected of you. You know that too well. It's how you've lived most of your life, living according to the strict social and moral codes of expected behaviour as a priest, a man of God, a man of the church, esteemed in the community. If you want to see Sonya, the only thing to do is to pretend that I've become best friends with Sonya."

"Pretend?"

"No, Sonya, don't get me wrong. Of course, you are my dear friend already. What I mean is that if you to want to be together, I'm going to have to be your chauffeur, baby-sitter, and chaperone, at least until Malachy is right before the church. So, I will spend a lot of time with you Sonya and invite you about so that it looks quite natural for Malachy to be with us both, simply as my brother."

"Fine, sister dear. But you have only three more weeks of holiday, then you are off and away again. I have four more weeks after that before my three months leave from the church expires, and a final decision must take place. What am I to do during this time?"

"That's your problem." She didn't mean to sound uncaring. With a softer tone, she said, "what are you going to do? As you've always done these last thirty-four years, dear brother, pray and restrain yourself."

"Fionnuala, you refuse to take me seriously."

"Oh, that's where you're wrong, dear brother, I am taking you very seriously. I am protecting your reputation." Her face expressed some of the increasing frustration she was experiencing. There was little doubt in her mind that his behaviour was unbecoming for his social and religious position.

"You know the situation is quite different now that I've met Sonya."

"Which brings the topic back to me. You both keep forgetting that I see enormous problems with Malachy's predicament, and I am no readier to commit myself to a forbidden romance than I am to fly to the moon."

"Maybe you will Sonya, my dear."

"Malachy, don't." The tone in Sonya's voice was resolute. The look on her face was final. Her face looked harsh.

"Don't what?"

"Heck, Malachy."

"I beg your pardon?" Malachy was lost, out of depth.

"Don't be bloody pretentious, Malachy. All I'm saying is that I don't want you to call me any endearments and don't assume we'll draw close." From tenderly repeating his name in his arms, Sonya had changed back into the stern, tense woman she'd become. The change came like lightning. Her body language made her appear formidable.

"Then you're playing him along, Sonya. If he can't assume anything from you, then you've closed your mind to him. You'll use him now, then dump him. I imagine that it's a bit exciting to be in the arms of a man who shouldn't be holding you. Not that I'd know, but when it becomes scandalised, you'll run like a deer away from the strife. He can't run. Don't do it Sonya, there's too much at stake for Malachy to have any woman trifle with his emotions, only to leave him dangling and destroyed. There's much more at stake for Malachy to explore love, than with any ordinary man. The point of contention is that he's not an ordinary man. This is a forbidden love."

"A forbidden love? Is that what you think?" Both women ignored these questions and the hurt look on Malachy's face. Their immediate fight was with each other.

"Fionnuala that's exactly my point. I'm not playing Malachy along. I am not trifling with anyone's emotions. I've resisted Malachy's charms and held back."

"Too true."

"But you are a priest Malachy, what else did you expect from me?"

"Were a priest, that's right."

"Are a priest dear brother, you still are a priest. Don't forget it. You forget it at your peril. And Sonya, I don't exactly see you resisting

Malachy's abundant charms. You lap them up like you're starved for excitement. You're messing around with his emotions and that angers me."

"This is a mess." Sonya looked for a seat and flopped down.

"It doesn't have to be a mess."

"Only if it turns out your way Malachy. Otherwise, you're left embarrassed, ashamed, and a disgrace to yourself, your sister, your village, and I imagine to your seminary. You can't let that happen; you mustn't let it happen. Forget about me, it's easier that way."

Deep down, Fionnuala knew that her brother was dogged. None of his behaviour made sense to her, but she'd seen the look of determination on his face the second she had arrived home. He had changed, a woman had brought this change, an unknown, beautiful woman had entered his life. Building on her knowledge of his character, she said, "Malachy, there's a lot to be discussed before you plunge in. You've been used to giving everyone else advice over the years. Now it's your turn to receive it. A widow and a priest. I'm not sure that I'm ready for the combination. You now must take advice yourself. We mustn't have a scandal of any sort."

"I'm not adverse to taking advice Fionnuala, you know that. I seek help from Paddy frequently. Arrogance has never been part of my personality. But in the realm of romantic love, obviously I am a babe in the wood compared to you women of the world," and his eyes sparkled, hoping in vain to create a lighter atmosphere in the room, "but I am excited about exploring love. You women can think what you want. As day turns into night, as the sun sets and rises, as we're all born and eventually die, I know what I'm saying. I am in pursuit of love."

Sonya was uncomfortable. Ready to change the orientation of the conversation, she stood up. "Have you seen around the place?"

"No, we respected your privacy. We were only in the kitchen and took a quick trip into the bedroom to find your clothes."

"Come, I want to show you around."

"Are you sure?" Malachy reached a hand, squeezed it affectionately, but Sonya ignored the gesture and thrusting his hand aside, lead the way.

She was entering new territory.

Seven

Curiously, Sonya began the tour of her house by taking them back toward the front door. With their backs to the old pine scrub door, they looked down into a large open plan room that contained a comfortable lounge suite covered with an ethnic print fabric. Bookshelves filled with novels and lavish art books lined several walls, and a study desk sat under the window. The room was tastefully and artistically decorated with large pots, candles, lamps, and framed art strategically placed to maximise their aesthetic appeal.

From where they stood, there were uninterrupted glorious vistas of the garden, the rugged clifftop, and the turbulent ocean. Glass windows encircled the entire frontage of the room, as well as around the front left side where the dining room looked out. Immediately left, Sonya opened a door quickly and they saw it was another entrance into the kitchen. To the front left, she walked them into the open dining area where they'd already been. From here, they went down a few stairs into another level. Her crutches helped her. Two front rooms again had uninterrupted spectacular views. She walked them quickly into her bedroom.

Malachy mentally noted the king-size bed and walked up almost reverentially to examine the large portrait of a man on the wall. It was obviously Malcolm. "He looks a very content man."

Not replying, Sonya moved into the next room. A delightful

conservatory full of lush plants obviously in need of some immediate care opened out into the garden. Looking up from the conservatory, you could see into the lounge. They took the steps back up. Sonya was handling these better than she had expected.

To the front right side of the lounge was an artist delight, a spacious room, again with fabulous views and wonderful light, an artist's asset. This room alone had convinced Sonya to buy the cottage. The light was sharp and continuous, and the views an inspiration. Sonya's paints, easels, and brushes lay in evident order, clear to an artist.

Sonya pulled on Fionnuala's arms as if this was the easy part of the tour. Without saying a word, she made it clear that the only thing to do was to go the whole way, to show them the whole house, and to get it over and done with. With visible frustration, she said, "come on. You can look at the paintings another time."

She took them back to the front door and stood trembling. "What's wrong Sonya?" Fionnuala asked kindly.

"As you can see, I have wonderful views from every room. I can see out, but no one wandering by can see in." Trying to be evasive, she stood leaning on the door, breathing deeply.

"One more room Sonya, why is opening the door troubling you?"

Sonya cast a furtive glance at Malachy. How had he known there was one more room and that the idea of going in upset her deeply? Surely, he couldn't know her this well so quickly. She hadn't realised that she kept looking at the door to the right, then looking far out to sea, in a repetitive fashion, avoiding going in.

"Whatever's in there, we don't have to go in," and the soothing voice of Fionnuala rushed over her like a breath of wind. She was thoughtful. Strengthened in some way by this knowledge that what she was about to do was a conscious choice to take her visitors in, that she could have chosen to avoid this room, she turned the handle deliberately, breathed audibly, and opened it fully.

Malachy and Fionnuala tiptoed in as if they were entering a shrine. In many ways, they were in a shrine, a temple to the dead, a place to come and sit and remember. The room had two single beds, one made up in a very feminine lavender spotted duvet cover with frilly pink pillows. This bed was covered with carefully dressed dolls and teddy bears. The other bed had a fire engine duvet cover and teddies lay strategically alongside of little toy cars. These were obviously the sentimental belongings of her dear children, now gone. There was hardly a scrap of wallpaper that could be seen. The walls were covered densely with picture frames of her wedding photos, baby pictures, art scribbles the children had done, family photos, school certificates, and all sorts of precious memorabilia.

There was no conversation. Sonya sat on Katie's bed. Fionnuala stood by Matthew's bed, taking in the broad scenario, turning slowly to enable her to see the pictures. Malachy crept around the room like a detective, examining the photos closely, and periodically glancing back at Sonya who stoically stared at the ground as if she was seeing nothing, then he went back to scrutinise minute detail.

A stranger walking in at this moment might have been surprised at the next reaction. Fionnuala ran out crying and curled herself up into a foetal ball and lay on the sofa sobbing. Sonya didn't have the inner resources to comfort her. She hobbled out stiffly and went into the kitchen to find bread and cheese for lunch. Malachy stayed in the room. Sometime later, as Sonya was seeking help to lay food on the table, Malachy went across to his sister, and wordlessly, sat stroking her. This brought back peculiar memories to Sonya. Malachy walked across to Sonya.

"Shut that door," she screamed at him.

Bewildered, he looked around him, not knowing exactly what she was referring to. "There's no need to scream."

"Shut that door," she screamed again.

Malachy was accustomed to peace and dialogue. The sound of a woman screaming at him was foreign. It disturbed him, and with one look at his sister, he knew that it had frightened Fionnuala. She was abundantly good-natured. Sonya hobbled over and shut the door herself.

Malachy walked over to her and held her clenched fists tightly, and said, "there was no need to scream at me. Cry Sonya, cry."

"No, I've done my crying." Her body was stiff and unyielding.

"Maybe you haven't Sonya. You're so tense. You didn't have to scream at me like that."

His touch had an immediate soothing effect. There was something magical about his hands on hers, and she wanted to throw herself onto his shoulders, to have his arms hold her securely again, but she felt bad, that again, she had been harsh, when he had been nothing but kind to her. Clearly, she wasn't ready to be loved. At this precise moment, she could understand why Fionnuala thought she was playing with his charms.

Lunch was a quiet occasion. Malachy voiced some of his concerns gently. "Sonya, I wonder if it would be more sensible to spread your photos throughout the house."

"What do you mean?" How quickly annoyance shot into her voice. The speed of aggravation worried Fionnuala tremendously.

"You have everything sentimental concentrated in one room, except for the picture of Malcolm in your bedroom. It must be a nightmare when you go into that bedroom."

"A nightmare? You really don't have a clue." Sonya's face was hot and flushed and spoiled her appearance.

"I'm sorry?" Malachy wasn't clear what she meant.

"A nightmare? That room is my source of joy."

"Maybe it was your source of joy, but I also think it's part of your source of pain."

Sonya clammed up. Like an oyster preparing a pearl, she refused to open her mouth. Fionnuala sympathised with her brother. She liked Sonya, but she feared her quick temper, and Malachy didn't deserve the anguish of having to endure lashings of harsh words. He was born good-natured. He had been nothing but tender and considerate to this woman. Fionnuala had observed his continual acts of compassion. He never lost his cool with her, years of patient training in self-control and giving pastoral counsel to others had prepared him well.

"I'll clear away," she volunteered, hoping the chance to be alone would give them a few moments to restore emotional equilibrium. She noticed how Malachy's touch soothed Sonya. She hoped that whatever he did, he would be discreet, and that things would work out well for them both. There was no way she wanted her dear brother to suffer at the hands of this woman who moved from warmth to icy chilliness in a frightening flash.

Malachy was a wise man. He took Sonya by the elbow, lead her across to the sofa, placed her crutches on the ground, pushed her down gently, and wrapped his arms around her. He placed her head on his chest, and slowly felt her head relax into his arms. He waited for some time, until he felt that she was calmer, then with a finger on her chin, he lifted her face upward toward his. Their eyes met, held, and wouldn't be distracted. He moved nearer to her, so that his lips were almost touching hers. He wanted to be sure that this was what she wanted, as well as what he wanted. But he was inexperienced in these matters.

Certainly, he'd watched films, observed the screen hero overcome the heroine with his touch, watched his friends, but now, he felt hesitant. Sonya sensed this hesitation. She moved to make contact. What a sweet first kiss, brief, but oh so beautiful. She moved away, then their lips met again, and as if nature took its own course, Malachy was master. Oh, this was heaven! This woman's lips were doing things to his body that years of celibacy had forbidden.

"Oh Sonya, my darling."

"Malachy, Malachy, Malachy."

"Sorry to interrupt you again but let me remind you that this type of thing is going to happen time and time again. I'm here to interrupt you, and to nudge you back into the real world. Believe me, my task is not a fun one."

Sonya sat back in Malachy's arms as if she was meant to be there. It was a place to feel safe in. Fionnuala felt awkward in her brother's presence. Obviously, she wasn't accustomed to seeing him holding a woman. It didn't seem right. She could see his priestly dog collar which he wore when he went out in public or knew that people were coming to his house. Despite priding herself on being a tolerant, liberal woman, it seemed decidedly wrong. She'd been in many men's arms, but Malachy was different. He was a man chosen by God to live apart from women. What he was doing now was forbidden. With good reason.

On Malachy's request, they spent the afternoon looking through photo albums. He insisted on starting from Sonya's baby photos, hoping to find out as much about her as possible. It was a hilarious time as Sonya showed her baby, toddler, and girlhood days in sunny California. Next came her days at art college, and various boyfriends appeared on the scene. She turned some pages quickly. Loud, raucous laughs exploded with every new outlandish fashion, until Malcolm appeared, and Sonya's mood changed instantly. There was no anger or irritability, just a hushed sadness. She closed the books.

Fionnuala couldn't help but notice how easy Malachy's touch was. For a man who'd never touched a woman, he was free with his caresses. It gave her the creeps to watch him. It wasn't natural. He was a priest. He left his hand on her knee, slid it up to her thigh, and laughed so joyously and heartily that he was almost lying on her lap. More than once she saw his lips brush over her hair.

All this affectionate touch might be alright in acceptable normality, but her brother didn't live a normal life. If he became used to this touch, how would he discipline himself when he was in public? Was he pursuing the right path? He didn't even know this woman properly. She might have a disturbed streak; she might turn nasty on him. They'd witnessed her temper, chilly iciness, and tight withdrawal. He was moving far too fast. It wasn't exactly her business, but her brother's matters had always been part of her life, until now. She felt isolated and wondered if she was being unreasonable.

"Come on Malachy, we have to be off." Space away from this peculiar intimacy was what she wanted to clear her throbbing head.

"Yes, yes, in good time."

"No, now."

This insistence wasn't typical. Fionnuala was usually flexible and spontaneous. Malachy swivelled around to observe his sister's face and wasn't sure what he read in her lines of worry. Hustling things together, Fionnuala signalled that she was ready to leave. Malachy was confused at her sudden change of temperament but accepted that her chauffeur identity was important to building his relationship with Sonya, and that he must keep his sister happy.

"So, you'll come to our place tomorrow, Sonya," he said.

"Yes, Malachy, that's arranged already. Come on, we're leaving now."

"You go on."

"No Malachy, we have to leave together. It's broad daylight. You can't be seen coming out later by yourself. You might want risky games, but I will not have a scandal." Her tone was insistent.

"I think you're being overly cautious."

"That's a joke! There's no such thing around here, and you know that as well as I do." Fionnuala was not giving them any more time to be alone. She was troubled with the pace that Malachy was moving. Now, her attitude was that anything that had to be said or done, had to be said or done in her presence. Yes, she would censor whatever she felt needed censorship. She loved her brother, and while she didn't live here anymore, she adored her village ties.

Malachy stood up, held Sonya in his arms, and said, "please let your hair tumble down tomorrow, just for me."

She smiled. "Tomorrow."

"Promise?"

"I promise."

Malachy kissed her softly on the lips, a new experience for him, a luscious pleasure for her. He left and she was alone with her thoughts and with the cherished recollections of his arms around her, his body close to hers, and his lips on hers. What delightful recollections to have! What spoiled it all was her quick, impatient temper. Wanting and not wanting, not knowing what she wanted, or what she despised, made her feel giddy. She knew that this giddiness was no excuse for her frosty attitude or her erratic moods.

On the trip back, both Malachy and Fionnuala were talking about the same sorts of things. They were shocked by Sonya's temper, her screams, and the rapid change of moods. They wondered how wise it was to have one room where she could go to be haunted by the past, and to relive old memories. The room was overflowing with memorabilia, so full that they thought it unbearably impossible to cope with. Then, with her fierce need to shut the door on the room, it was as if she was trying to keep the pain at bay, when all she did, was keep the torment tight inside her.

Could Malachy help to release this pain? Was it appropriate that he try?

Eight

Sonya spent a refreshing night back in her own home. The nightmares that had frequently kept her from sleeping didn't come back to obsess her. Instead, she slept with the remembrance of Malachy's arms around her. For the first time since the horrible accident, she felt herself becoming a whole woman again. Someone wanted her. Not just anyone, but someone who declared he was looking for love. She couldn't rush her own feelings; they weren't clear yet. Her quick flashes of fiery temper dampened the fire she felt in her belly.

But just as she was getting used to the idea of being reassured again, an unmistakable bewilderment crept in like an unwanted stranger in the night. Malachy had more at stake in pursuing love than she did. There was no doubt about that. And she certainly didn't know what she felt for him or if she'd ever love him. Fionnuala was quite right in this matter of the stakes of love.

Sonya had no intention of playing games with Malachy, but she didn't want to rush into something that she wasn't sure of. Oh, she loved his touch, the merest caress on her was enough to make her shiver with delight, but that was not love. She knew that. Having been a married man's mistress, she recognised there was a significant difference between lust and love. What the next weeks would bring, she couldn't be certain.

Meanwhile, Malachy woke after a blissful night of sleep. He had dreamt vividly of Sonya dancing naked through a field of daffodils and moving nearer toward him. Oh, how seductive she looked, flicking her hair across her breasts, then throwing it away off her shoulders, exposing herself fully, without any need of shame. He was lying naked on a rug, the sun shining on his solid, firm body gleaming with a sweaty desire. As she fell onto him, pressing her breasts into his chest, they embraced in a loving embrace that made him waken with sensations he'd not experienced since he was a teenager. He felt mildly embarrassed, but mostly amused. He'd have a lot of adjustments to make in this life.

Accustomed to early rising for morning prayers, a lie in bed with lustful fantasies was a far cry from his everyday priestly experiences. He welcomed the newness with his arms outstretched and with his athletic body feeling invigorated. Life was good. He arose early and opened his Bible.

He longed to hear Sonya's American voice again, but he'd never seen her use a phone. Surely, she had one somewhere. He had already thought that the one way they would be able to maintain regular contact unseen by prying, suspicious eyes, unheard by over-eager gossipers, would be on the phone. Bother! The mobile phone coverage in their area had improved, most of the older locals didn't bother, but he heard the frustration of the younger ones when their signal wavered.

Fionnuala had something planned for the morning. She was being rather secretive about it. He suspected it had something to do with Sonya, because his sister had insisted that she would pick her up and bring her back to lunch. Something to do with proprietary and being seen to be doing the right things was his sister's official reason.

Malachy thought back dismally to last night. They had had a terrible row over Sonya and his priestly vocation. Fionnuala had repeatedly sermonised him on letting people down, and being sure of the right decisions, and not rushing into anything too quickly. Fionnuala was very concerned with Sonya's moodiness and quick rage, and the fact that Malachy knew so little about her background, or the sort of woman she was.

Malachy understood her concern but saw the moody rage as part of necessary adjustments Sonya was making in moving from a life of tragic loss and pain to a future of hope and joy. They were both sad at the end of the night. They rarely fought or bickered. There were big changes going on in them both. He felt sure they'd work something positive out in the long run, but he knew that it would be a matter of time, and time wasn't something he had on his side. Three months in a lifetime was a short stretch to make a decision that was as crucial as the one he was about to make.

He was clear about it though. In many ways, he had already made the decision. He craved intimacy. He could still work in the church, although never again as a priest. Of course, this was a sad decision, as well as a grave choice, but it was an enormous resolution he had made, after wrestling in prayer. And he had made it in good conscience, a man at peace with himself and with his God.

He was also a man privately amused with the vividness of his fantasy life that now preoccupied much of his daytime as well as his dream life. The transition from total inexperience, ignorance, and indifference to arousal, experimentation, and desire, was rapid. He took it in his stride. This was the direction his new life would go. He was happy about it. Malachy began this morning with zest.

Fionnuala was subdued over breakfast. The mood of the prior evening was carrying over into the next morning, although they bore each other no grudges.

"See you later," she called over her shoulder, away early. He went off on his morning jog, keeping his supple body well-toned.

Fionnuala drove straight to Sonya's cottage. "Oh Sonya, you look beautiful," she commented as Sonya came bounding on crutches to the door, just as soon as she heard the car driving up. "Malachy will be bowled over when he sees you. He'll not be able to contain himself for one second. His hands will go roaming everywhere they shouldn't be going."

"I decided it was time to dress more like I used to dress. It does seem unusual though. It was easier than finding any trousers that could be pulled over my leg." The entire time she had lived in the village, Sonya had worn nothing but dark, drab jeans, oversized men's shirts, and long, unbecoming jumpers. The shirts came from Malcolm's wardrobe. She'd brought them with her.

"You look gorgeous."

Sonya looked down at herself and felt shy. She had put on a waisted dress with a scooped neckline. Its cream colour with pastel floral print softened her appearance considerably. She wore a pale blue ballet shoe on her one good leg. "Halfway there with my hair," she joked as she swung around and flicked her ponytail in front.

"We'll get it down and flowing yet," Fionnuala laughed. "There is something else different about you today. Your complexion is amazingly subtle."

"It's make-up. I can't believe it. It's been ages since I bothered to put on make-up, and I felt like I was painting a picture. Americans wear piles of make-up, so too did many women when I was living in Belfast. My art students wore layers of black eye make-up, and many adopted a gothic style. I grew up smearing the stuff on. When I first came to the island of Ireland, I couldn't believe it. I've seen some women who wear stacks of make-up but lots of women don't wear any. I compromised and enjoyed not wearing much around the home or into art college, then I loved to dress up glamorously at night. But I've not worn a spot of make-up, not even a stroke of lipstick since the funeral."

Off they went together to the jaunt they had planned on the last day in hospital. At least, Fionnuala had planned it, and Sonya had agreed to it. "You look lovely Sonya, as I keep saying. In fact, you look sensational. No one will recognise you. I'll enjoy showing you off." All memories of the argument the night before with her brother had faded well into the background. Or at least, she made sure it stayed hidden in the background. She was a gracious, considerate woman.

"Will I be alright?"

"Where?"

"In the hairdressers with all the locals?"

"You'll be the star attraction. Just take it in your stride. I made two bookings, there'll be expecting to cut the sacred hair of the good Father O'Sullivan. They'll die with fright and excitement when they see you walk in with me. The word will go out that not only is the American woman in the hairdresser's salon, but she's looking like a film star. 'Quick, come and see her curls cascading down her backs,' they'll say to everyone they see. They'll be selling tickets to let people queue up to see you."

They laughed heartily. Fionnuala was skilled at putting people at their ease. "You exaggerate, surely."

"You really don't know how small villages operate do you? Just wait and see."

With some trepidation, Sonya got out of the car, and not even noticing anyone else, she followed Fionnuala in. She was relieved to be in her company. Fionnuala was happily chatting to all and sundry as if she came into the hairdressers with Sonya frequently.

"A complete cut for me, a condition treatment for Sonya and a two-centimetre trim for her. Now, have you got that straight, did you hear me correctly? I said two-centimetres only, not a hairsbreadth more, that's exactly what I mean." People jumped to attention, she had a persuasive command over people, softened by her charm, not unlike that of her brother.

Everyone was chatting, laughing, giggling, asking Sonya questions, expecting answers, and looking at her, discretely and explicitly. Having been out of all normal social life for such a long time, Sonya was overwhelmed by the noise and the attention that she was receiving. Fionnuala was right, a lot of people seemed to be coming into the village today and it wasn't even market day. Word must have travelled quickly, as any word in a small village can do. An abnormally high number of people came in to make appointments at the hairdressers.

Sonya smiled to herself, at least she was stimulating trade. She was forever grateful for Fionnuala's presence. Every time a tricky question came up that related to her personal family background, or every time she sensed that Sonya felt awkward, Fionnuala directed the conversation back to neutral territory. She knew the villagers well.

Sitting under the dryer, Sonya let her thoughts drift off to the man she would see soon. She loved the idea of it. She treasured the new zest for life he had given her. She vowed to keep her temper under control. This irritability was a baffling aspect of their relationship, not something that she was prone to. Normally, she was calm, and in the past, she could manage a family, children, teaching, painting, and running a household without being unduly flustered. But that was before the darkness had descended on her, crushing her spirit.

Adjustments to new situations and to different people had never seemed as awkward to her. It was only now as she was re-entering social life that she started to accept that in avoiding counsellors and therapists after the accident, she'd lost the chance to work through her grief immediately. Hiding herself away as she'd done hadn't worked. It simply had buried the pain deeper. Sonya was jolted back to reality by the hairdresser who'd removed the dryer and was combing out her stunning locks.

"So, you've got Father O'Sullivan to thank for a lot of things, have you now?" The hairdresser asked the question pointedly.

"Mm," she agreed.

"Ah, now isn't he just the finest man you could have had to rescue you?" The woman smiled knowingly, her eyes sparkling.

Sonya played it safe. "Mm," she agreed again.

The hairdresser leaned down, and whispering she said, "awful good-looking isn't he just?"

"Mm."

"By Jaysus, ain't he such a looker! Whew!" And the girl whistled under her breath. "What about his body? Isn't he a magnificent specimen? Bit wasted on a priest, isn't it?" When no answer came, she continued, "you know what I mean, don't you?" The smirk told all.

Sonya was more flustered by the girl's comments than she should have been, but the constant comings and goings in the salon, and her sitting like an exhibit in an art show, had caught up on her, and now threatened to overwhelm. It was an enormous relief when she could say thank you to everyone and leave the salon.

Back in the car, Fionnuala laughed non-stop for the first five minutes. She had overheard all the conversations and questions directed toward Sonya and had read the double meanings into all of them.

"You handled that well, my friend. Seriously, Sonya, your hair is a triumph of nature. It is the sort of hair that old-time grandmothers used to call a 'crowning glory'. If I had your hair, I'd never tie it back. It would flow down my back for the whole world to see every single day. I don't know how my dear brother Malachy is going to behave with you. You look like an angel."

"Believe me, I am not one." Her smile was more a grimace.

"I hope I'm not intruding, but I want to watch Malachy's face when he first sees you, then I'll disappear for a while." Sonya said nothing. "Is that all right?"

"Yes."

"What's wrong?"

"Nothing."

"That's not true."

"I feel nervous."

"That's healthy."

This was the first time that Malachy would see her hair flowing nicely. When she was unconscious in his cottage, it had been tied back.

Malcolm had adored her hair, she suspected that Malachy would too.

Nine

The closer they got to the cottage, the more nervous Sonya felt. She wanted Malachy to ravish her and sweep her into his arms, but she was terrified of letting him down later. It wasn't fair to take his caresses and then to hurl them back in his face later. The present and the future merged in a jumbled mess. Pain and loss mangled with the elusive possibility of hope and gain.

Fionnuala swept her quickly inside, shutting the door behind them both. "Malachy," she called, "we're back."

He came running down the corridor into the hall. One look at Malachy's face told Fionnuala everything, and she discreetly left the hall quicker than she'd intended doing. Instead of sweeping her off her feet as Sonya had expected, Malachy stood from a distance staring at her as if she was a ghost.

"Malachy." Her voice was tentative.

"Sonya." Uncharacteristically, there was no emotion in his voice. He didn't move.

"How do I look Malachy?" This is a question Sonya never asked. She had never posed this question in her entire life, not even once to a girlfriend, loathing other women who did. Her line was that a compliment sought is not worth the compliment given. She despised herself for asking it. What was happening to her? It made her sound vain, and she wasn't that sort of person. But she was impatient for a response. Malachy was standing statue-like, firmly erect, a long way away from her. She wanted him to rush to her, sweep her into his arms, hug, caress, and shower her with his kisses.

Instead, he covered his face with his hands as if he couldn't bear to look at her. "Sonya."

Misinterpreting him completely, Sonya was devastated. "Malachy, what's wrong?" Her face was distorted with heartfelt anguish.

In response, Malachy walked slowly to her, step-by-step, dragging time, his eyes holding her with the strength of a powerful force. He stood a body distance from her, then with one hand, he dramatically picked up a handful of golden hair and let it drop. With the other hand, he reverentially picked up another handful of soft hair and let it drop also. With one hand under her throat, and the other hand on the back of her hair, he crushed her to him, and kissed her with an intensity of craving he had never felt in his life.

It was like she was falling onto him as in a dream. For Sonya, it was impossible to believe that this man hadn't kissed a woman before. He was masterful. The thrill that surged through her being was what she relished.

"My God Sonya, you are unbelievably beautiful. Your hair is like an angel's hair," and again he picked up little handfuls, brought them to his face to smell their salon freshness and feel their softness against his rougher skin. He turned around so that he could see the full effect of her curls cascading down her back.

"So, you've seen my hair now Malachy. When I first saw your face, I didn't know what you are thinking. You looked awestruck, like you were staring at my naked body."

He laughed, more to himself than with her. The vividness of his dream was still alive. "It felt like I was staring at your naked body. Your hair exposes you. It was like you are open for me to see through your layers. And my God, you're perfectly beautiful, and this dress is gorgeous." He ran a finger around her round neckline. She loved it. The lightness of his touch was charged with such an energy flow that her entire being felt captivated. They moved easily into each other's arms, and their lips found each other as if they were meant to be together.

Fionnuala, walking into the room on this occasion, felt alienated from her brother, realising she'd have to get used to seeing him embrace this woman. Nevertheless, she was determined to pull them apart at this moment for the sake of her sanity and his integrity. "Come, come you too. We have windows for the world to see in, and I will just die if anyone catches you embracing like that."

The couple laughed, and they sat down to a delightful lunch of poached salmon and salad. Baby potatoes sat happily in melted butter and home-grown parsley. The women told Malachy of the fun, games, and embarrassment at the hairdresser's salon, and of the stream of questions Sonya had had to endure about why this was the first time she'd come to the salon, how did she break her leg, why was Fionnuala with her, could she manage her cottage with her crutches, what sort of painting did she do, and of course, how blessed she was that Father O'Sullivan had rescued her.

After lunch, Sonya insisted on reversing the pattern of the day before. She wanted to see their photo albums. Having been raised in comparative poverty to Sonya, they had few photos of early childhood, just bits and pieces taken by other relatives and some school and sport photographs. There were more photos of Fionnuala's time at university and Malachy's student days at the seminary. In these photos, Malachy looked austere and serious, a stranger to the relaxed, charming man sitting beside her. Fionnuala had loads of up-to-date photos on her iPhone of her journalistic career, but Malachy was not in these, and Sonya lost some interest.

Fionnuala did nothing to disguise her frustration. Malachy couldn't keep his hands off Sonya. Every time he walked past, he felt compelled to touch her. Sitting on the sofa together, they were almost on top of each other. Sonya looked breath-taking. Fionnuala wasn't jealous. She was a strong, attractive woman. She quite simply was worried about the sensibility of her brother, something she'd never had to worry about before.

Malachy's caresses weren't sensible, someone might see them, and shame would fall onto her for letting it happen. She had to look after him, mother him, if that was necessary. Malachy was moving too fast for her liking. The contrast between Father O'Sullivan celibate priest, and Malachy the lustful stimulated man, was extreme, too drastic to come to grips with in this short holiday. There'd been nothing to prepare her for this.

Sonya was lapping up Malachy's attention, a woman transformed by soaking up affection. Fionnuala couldn't cope with what she saw as the absurdity of falling for someone you did not know, and she left them together.

They lost no time. "Malachy, Malachy, Malachy."

"Yes, my lovely one?"

"I love the sound of your name."

"Do you love the taste of my kisses?" He swooped in to kiss her and as she moved back to grasp his head, unintentionally his head fell onto her chest. She held him close while he listened to her heartbeat quicken and felt her breathing rising and falling. Malachy could hardly kiss Sonya without such a desire rushing through him that he didn't know how to manage his urges, so he just sat holding her. He could not see what he ached to see. They sat still for a long stretch of time, not speaking, simply becoming accustomed to each other's body rhythms, breath, and touch.

In his mind, he had left the church, he was no longer a priest, although he still had some church commitments to carry out. But he would leave, he rationalised, it was only a matter of time. There was no need for him to feel guilt or shame at desiring this woman, or longing to see her body, and wanting to kiss and caress her. At least, that was the story he repeatedly told himself. He was honest enough to admit that his rationalisation didn't always feel proper.

He had lived a life of self-control and restraint. His sister's constant reminders that his actions were not right, nagged him. He'd always trusted her views. He knew she was partially correct, she usually was. They had no idea how much time had passed when Fionnuala came and reminded Malachy of a church task he had later that night. He felt safe with Fionnuala around. He had always looked after her, but now, she was his guardian, making sure that he didn't overstep the mark, or act provocatively or prematurely. His self-control was questionable. He knew it, he didn't need a sister to remind him with the frequency with which she did. These experiences were novel.

"I can take you home now, Sonya."

"You can't do that, Malachy." A tired frustration sounded in Fionnuala's voice.

"Why not?" Memories of their row the previous night flooded back again.

"How many times do we have to talk about it? You can't be seen leaving Sonya home. I have to do it."

"She's right, Malachy."

"Of course, I am right. You've got to live in the real world you two, and the real world is this village."

"What's your phone number, Sonya?"

"I'm not on the phone, and I haven't restarted a mobile phone account."

"Not on the phone?" Malachy paused, letting that sink in. "Why not?"

"Haven't you listened to anything these last weeks?" A slight tone of annoyance he hadn't heard this day crept back into her voice again.

"Yes, of course I've listened. What's that got to do with you not being on the phone?"

"I didn't want anyone to contact me, until now."

"But now you have a reason to get it on, you will, right?"

"No Malachy, I don't want it on."

"But you must have it on. I need you to be on the phone. I must be able to talk to you." There was desperation in his voice.

"I don't want it on." She repeated herself.

"Why not now?" Fionnuala was trying to mediate.

"Mainly because I don't want Malcolm's family ringing me. Their intentions are all noble, but I still need a lot of personal space. I want to choose who I speak to and when I speak to them. I don't want to re-live old times with them, which is what they'd want to do if they knew I was on the phone. They've lost a son, a grandson, and a granddaughter, and will want to reminisce. I can't do it, not yet. Perhaps a time will come when I can talk with them. It's easier for me not to bother with the phone."

"You wouldn't have to broadcast your number. You could just give it to me if you chose to. Please get it on for me." Malachy was despondent. He'd hoped that the phone would be his lifeline these next weeks. Fionnuala was right. He had to be discreet, he couldn't be seen visiting Sonya, and certainly never alone. He wanted the phone on. It had to be connected, or to begin a new mobile plan.

"Don't clam up on us again, Sonya."

"I won't, but I'm not ready for the intrusiveness of the phone yet."

"Intrusiveness?" Malachy couldn't believe what he was hearing. "Would making calls to you really be intrusive?"

"I'm not ready, Malachy."

"Not ready for my phone calls?" The man shook his head in disbelief. The ways of women were a puzzle. "Intrusive?" He shook his head again. "I don't believe this."

"I don't want to have to talk on the phone to anyone if I'm not in the right frame of mind." Fionnuala and Malachy shook their head. Their phones were their lifeline to each other, especially when Fionnuala was travelling abroad for work.

Fionnuala swept them aside and drove Sonya home. There was no need for talk. It would have been repetitive. Sonya was glad to be alone with her thoughts. It had been a full day. Hair salons, kisses, and talk of non-existent phones, what a curious combination.

As she sat in her bedroom, then sprawled loosely on the king-size bed trying to make sense of the day, every combination of confused thought raced through her muddled brain, from her curly hair to her daughter's curly hair, Malachy' kisses to remembering Malcolm's kisses. She gazed at his photo on the wall. She needed more time before she was ready to fully engage with the outside world.

Turning away from Malcolm's photo, Malachy's name spun out of control in the air. How could this relationship ever work? It couldn't, could it?

Ten

The peace of her bed was a wonder. It had been such an emotionally taxing day that Sonya fell asleep immediately with the fresh taste of Malachy's lips on hers. She woke revitalised, drew the curtains, took a quick glance at the photo of Malcolm as she had done every morning, added a quick but flirtatious bold thought about Malachy, and lay back in bed, looking far ahead of her.

Having such splendid views was a treat to her artist's eyes as well as to her troubled soul. Despite the major storm which suddenly seemed so long ago, her garden was blooming. It was alive with colour, flowers, shrubs, tall trees, and birdlife. She loved the freshness of different buds to greet her, and spring always burst onto the horizon with its new life. What would her new life bring? How novel was her new life?

She looked further to the end of the garden where an unshaped hedge grew behind her picket fence. A gate at the far-right corner led on to the cliff. Beside the house itself, this access gate had been a feature. She was the only one in the village who had direct access from her house to the cliffs, and her back gate led into a series of stairs down to the beach. It was almost like having a private beach. No one would use those stairs unless they were coming directly up the path into her back garden and into her house. When the tide was in, no one had access from the beach to the stairs, so she had no fear of people creeping up at night.

She thought back to her injury and how much had happened since that fateful day when she'd been out walking, had got a trifle tired, sat down by a tree, and fallen asleep. It was unlike her to act like this.

The next thing she had remembered was seeing a man in the shadow of the door frame. Often, she lay in bed thinking about him watching her asleep in his sister's bed. She respected his position enough to know that he would not have done anything dishonourable to her. Indeed, a man who claimed he could undress her and place a nightgown on her without once looking at her body was accomplished in being virtuous to a woman. But what went through his mind as he sat watching her? How often did he stroke her hair when she was asleep? She trusted him wholeheartedly and was enchanted at the idea that he had observed her from a distance, even though she must have been a tantalising temptation.

Thinking what might have been if Malachy had not found her was too much to even contemplate. Seamus had reminded her of this more than once. While she had thanked Malachy briefly, she suddenly felt ashamed, as if it was only now that she was beginning to realise the enormity of what had transpired, and that he had saved her life. Not only had he saved her physically, but he'd also rescued her emotionally.

Malachy had come unexpected into her life and woken in her re-minders of the delightful joy of an affectionate man in her life. While she was revelling in these thoughts, the complications of their situation flooded her, and she pulled the quilt over her face as if to hide away.

Why a priest? If she was to allow a man back into her life, why couldn't it have been someone safe like a bank manager, a school-teacher, or an accountant? Fate was complicated. Then she reminded herself that she'd done her long stretch of hiding, there was to be no more major hiding away in her new life. It was time to face the world and all it presented to her, no matter how difficult this might be.

The ocean caught her attention. How she loved the ocean. Paddling in its cool waters made her feel girlish again. She'd tried to swim, but it was freezing cold. She'd purchase a wetsuit. Watching the tides and the waves, reminded her of the movements of nature, that what goes out comes back in, but not always in the same form as before. Swimming and splashing in the ocean made her feel at one with the enormity of its hold over her. It was almost like a spiritual bond, a mermaid and the ocean, in mystical union.

As a painter, the changes in colour in the ocean thrilled her, the stimulating greens, the relaxing blues, and even the angry greys had their place in the total picture.

Thinking of angry greys prompted her to think of Malachy's cross words about the lack of a telephone, and this made her feel sad. He hadn't been irritable with her before, even though she'd been terribly cross with him, too many times. Was she being unreasonable about not having a phone put in? Perhaps his point was valid, that she didn't have to tell the world her number, indeed she could hold it back from everyone but him.

Word would get around, isn't that what Fionnuala was always saying? "You really don't know how a small village operates do you?" She heard Fionnuala's voice from yesterday as if she was standing there beside her now. Malachy had a point. Without the phone, their relationship was limited, particularly when Fionnuala left. He couldn't visit her every day. It wouldn't be proper. Did she want to stop Malachy from having contact with her? Truly, she wasn't sure what she wanted. That she wanted his body beside her, she was sure. His touch thrilled her. That she wanted his commitment, she was doubtful.

Clear reasons for her reluctance escaped her. There were doubts and confusions, and her emotions were sending mixed messages. The image of Malachy's body kept floating in front of her. He had a fantastic body, a body she was amazed at, one to look at, touch, and enjoy. The hair-dresser's apprentices knew exactly what they'd been talking about with their complementary whispers.

She didn't know why she felt such reluctance to be deeply involved. They knew very little about each other's past, hopes, and desires. Everything about their relationship was proceeding too quickly, and sensuality alone seemed to dominate. Time is what she needed to heal her emotional wounds of grief that still festered. The past kept being jumbled with the present that could not see toward the future. Indecision persisted.

The thought of a day without Malachy was not attractive. As a diversion, to chase away the emotional blues, she spent the morning trying on all the clothes she hadn't worn for a long time. Her bed was a mess, but she was having fun. Fun was something she had been very short of. Manoeuvring herself with a heavy cast on her leg wasn't easy. Frilly blouses, lacy underwear, sexy garters, silk stockings for her one good leg, and floral dresses lay strewn all over the bed.

She fingered the satin, silk, and lace, the sexy fabrics, these deliberately provocative fabrics, textiles that were meant to be fingered and felt. She began to imagine who was fingering them on her body. The cottons and the wools that she'd dressed herself in these last months were sensible, practical fabrics. Suddenly, she felt like tossing all her sombre garments out of the window. She wanted to wear every item of satin, silk, and lace that she possessed. She wanted tactile garments, and she knew who she wanted to be doing the sensual exploration of her body.

With the next outfit, she turned around to look at herself in the mirror, and gasped, she hardly recognised herself. This was a little black slinky number, a long smooth dress that she'd bought for exclusive events when she and Malcolm had dined out for special occasions. The dress had a plunging neckline. Her Wonderbra was doing the job that it promised to do, it gave her the ultimate cleavage. The back of the dress was also a deep plunging Vee.

This was the first time she'd looked at her body properly for months. She swirled around, feeling good about her body for the first time for ages. It was a firm, attractive body, well looked after, even though she'd had two children. Exercise was an important part of her life to maintain a supple body tone.

Today, in this outfit, she looked as sexy as she'd ever look, despite one leg still in plaster. She wanted Malachy to see her look like that, then she remembered, he was a priest. As if she was talking to him, she dramatically said to the mirror, "don't look, you're a priest."

Mimicking his melodious voice, she said, "was a priest don't you mean? It's only a matter of time, my lovely one," and she seductively wiggled her hips up to the mirror and jiggled her body. She had never been one to flaunt her body. It felt exciting. It was new. Pouting, she posed as if a photographer was about to capture her image. Oh, my word! Was this happening?

"Still are a priest," she said in Fionnuala's musical Irish voice. In defiance, she covered up some of her flesh.

Some movement in the distance caught her attention, and in disbelief, she gasped, "oh my God!" There, just about to open her back gate, was Malachy with another man. Both men were wearing clerical collars, so she presumed it was Father Tim, Malachy's good friend he kept talking about. "Clever man," she said to his vision walking up a back path, "you've come with another priest because that will look alright if anyone sees you." She struggled with her zip, startled as the men came closer. The more she panicked, the more the zip became tangled in the fine silky fabric. Her fingers fumbled in vain.

She heard a tap on the conservatory door, then when there was no answer, she heard a voice she normally would have been overjoyed to hear, call out, "Sonya? Where are you?" There was no way Sonya could get herself out of the dress. She couldn't find a shawl amidst the jumble on her bed. Suddenly feeling flustered, she couldn't find anything appropriate to throw over herself apart from the clothes lying sprawled over the bed. There was nothing left to do, but to swallow her pride and face these clerics. She found the crutches under a pile of clothes.

"My God Sonya!" was Malachy's first exclamation as she walked into the conservatory. "Cover yourself up." He was not entirely serious. His eyes were glued without shame to this sight of her delightful cleavage heaving up and down in embarrassment. No one was in doubt that he was turned-on by the moment.

The other man muttered, "hello," and turned away.

"Sonya, what's going on? Do you want to drive me to total distraction? Do you want me to ravish you in front of my best friend, the village priest?"

"Introductions, Malachy?"

"Introductions, Tim?" His voice was more high pitch than usual. "Explanations Sonya? How am I supposed to keep my eyes off you?"

"Your mate is managing well."

"He's not a raving lunatic priest in search of love."

"So, you've told him?"

Tim turned directly to her, and like a well-trained gentleman, as well as a priest, his eyes remained only on her face. "If Malachy won't introduce me, I will. I'm Father Tim O'Reilly, Tim to you. I know every trick this dear man has ever got into, every thought he's ever thought, and every..."

Malachy interrupted. "Tim kissed the Blarney Stone the day he was born, as you can hear. He's got the Irish gift of the gab, and likes to think he knows everything about me, but little does he know." They laughed companionably.

"Delighted to meet you Tim." Sonya felt instantly comfortable with Malachy's best friend. Again, he contradicted the stereotype she had about priests, especially Irish priests. He was Malachy's age, young, handsome, fresh, and light-hearted.

"Now Sonya, Tim may still have well-trained eyes. My eyes are out of control. You're a picture of beauty, but not the artistic, don't touch me, sort of beauty," and he ran his hands in the air making her shape. "My God Sonya, you are a sexy creature."

"Now now, Malachy, control my boy."

"I keep telling you my friend, I'm out of control."

"Look, I didn't know you were coming. I hardly put this dress on for the purpose of exciting your starved priestly eyes. I was trying clothes on that I'd not worn for ages. It's part of linking my past to the future. I had the dress on when I saw you wander up the garden path. I panicked and the zip is stuck. Can you help me Malachy?"

"Help a woman like you take off her dress? This is a new invitation.

I love it." He laughed, a wonderful, infectious tinkling laugh. Tim was laughing now, not at all phased by this experience. Indeed, he was clearly enjoying himself.

"Come on Malachy, help me." Sonya, while amused, was desperate to have the dress come off. She was feeling a bit stupid. She turned her back to him. Malachy was all fingers and thumbs. The mere touch of her body felt through the flimsy material and his fingers were rendered useless. To reach the zip, he had to put his hand down her back, that plunging, inviting Vee. Sonya was sweating in panic. Malachy's hands roamed uselessly, and then helplessly came back to the stuck zip, which stubbornly refused to budge.

She sat down on a couch, looked at these two men, and saw the strange humour in the situation. They all laughed heartily. Tim, in formal proprietary, never once dropped his eyes where it shouldn't be. Malachy allowed his eyes to stray freely, and in appreciation of the opportunity to do so, coming back to Sonya's seductive cleavage.

"Sonya, would you allow me to help you?" Tim came across to Sonya who stood up and turned her back to him, while he deftly loosened the zip, and then did it up correctly.

"How did you do that?" Sheer amazement was in his friend's voice.

"Easy Malachy. I used to do it often for my mother, God rest her soul." He crossed himself as was custom. "It was one of the few delights of the flesh I was allowed. Her arthritic fingers couldn't reach her zips. Dad made it clear to her that he would never bother with a woman's clothes. I was a grand hand at my sisters' tangled zips too. Also, and more obviously, I was calm." He said this with a Cheshire cat grin.

"I sure was not."

"That would have been obvious to the village idiot, not that we have one."

"Excuse me, while I change," and Sonya hurried as quickly as her leg would allow her, back to the bedroom to put on something more appropriate. She kept the Wonderbra on, pulled a white gently scooped bodysuit over it, and a long pink shirt with buttons. At the last moment, she undid several of the last buttons. She hoped she wouldn't regret this. Pulling on a long loose cream skirt, she took a quick look in the mirror, and knew that Malachy would like the smooth sensuality of her outfit.

"Coffee gentleman?" she asked as if nothing had happened. They grinned their assent.

"Sonya, my love, you look gorgeous in whatever you're wearing."
"Sh."
"What do you mean, sh? You're sounding like Fionnuala now."
"You know what I mean."
"What do you mean, Sonya?"
"Well Tim, I'm not sure what you know."
"Everything."

"This man likes to think he's God." The men had such an easy, jovial relationship, that it was hard to remember they were priests, except for the obvious sign of their priestly collars, and for Malachy's noticeable restraint in not pawing over Sonya every second possible.

"I was saying Tim, that the more Malachy calls me affectionate names and touches me here at home, the more likely he is to slip on the names and touch me in public, and that would be such a mistake."

"Aye, it would. But I think you can trust Malachy to be sensible in public."

"Ha," she snorted, "Malachy sensible? Do you see his wildly roaming hands? And him a priest! I'm not sure it's possible for him to be sensible." She was enjoying herself.

And as if to answer this jocular comment, Malachy came over, and unhassled by his mate's presence, seemingly more relaxed than in Fionnuala's company, he embraced Sonya provocatively, snuggling up to her. He went to kiss her, she knew not where precisely, but she thrust him aside.

Kisses were not for show, certainly not in front of Father O'Reilly.

Eleven

Sonya bustled about preparing food for lunch. She was getting used to using just one crutch in the kitchen. As they chatted easily, a bond was developing between the three very different individuals. Tim was jovial and an interesting conversationalist.

After lunch, they relaxed on the sofa. Malachy reached over to hold Sonya's hand. As he moved closer, his other hand rested on her thigh where her skirt flap had opened. She thrust his hands aside. She felt peculiar with Tim present. Malachy could pretend he was not a priest, but he was, and Sonya couldn't pretend he wasn't, even if Tim appeared relaxed about the two being together.

"Tim, this really is hasty of Malachy, isn't it?"

"What's the 'this' you're referring to?"

"You know."

"I have to say it's very different for me to see Malachy sit there with you. Lucky devil!" He laughed. "In all seriousness, we've talked long and hard about his situation, his decision, and the gravity of it all."

"And we've prayed together," added Malachy.

"Yes, and hard as it is, I've come to accept it, perhaps easier than I'd have imagined I would. But he's given me hints over these last few years that one day, something like this might happen to him. It hasn't come out of the blue. We've talked about this as a hypothetical. You know, the half drunken conversations that start, 'what if?' Or, 'imagine that I....,' you know, the sort of speculation I mean. I'm accepting his decision better than Fionnuala is. She had no hint of it coming, so she's in a state of shock. Our regular conversations had prepared me. But having said all this, I can't stress how important it is that no one, and I mean no one, has the slightest hint about it."

The late afternoon came on quickly. "You'll have to leave soon," Sonya said, "that's if you want to go home the coastal route. At this time of the year, the tide comes in quickly, and then you can't get down the stairs properly." She stared to the distant horizon. "Oh, how I miss the beach. I can't wait for my leg to be out of this heavy plaster cast because I'm dying to go down and feel my feet on the sand again."

"Sonya my love, you must promise me not to go on the beach until I can help you down the steps."

"Yes."

"I mean it, promise me?"

"I have."

"Sonya, there are two more things we wanted to ask you."

"We?"

"Yes, they both concern us and you."

"Us and you? You and me? Tim, my life is complicated enough with Malachy. Surely you're not about to join in?"

"Not like that." His laughter concealed mixed emotions. "Sonya, will you come to the pub on Saturday?"

"An innocent enough question. What's the big deal?"

"Yes, seemingly innocent, but can you, do it? Can you sit there with Malachy and the village residents and act as if Malachy means no more to you than the rest of us?"

"He doesn't, does he?" Sonya and Tim laughed, then sobered instantly at Malachy's grim face.

"What a serious face you have, Malachy."

"You really aren't taking me at my word Sonya, are you? This is no light game. This is the end game. This is not about a furtive fondle in the conservatory, followed by a kiss and a cuddle on the sofa, and see you later. This is my life. Yes, I am serious."

"Yes, and this is my life too. No less serious than yours, just very different. I have known love and sex and bodies and attraction, and I know you don't rush into anything as serious as a committed relationship."

"I'm not rushing."

"Not rushing?"

"Should I leave?"

"No Tim, stay. All our farewells seem to end like this, arguing or disagreeing over something. This is no different to usual."

Silence hovered heavily. Tim broke it. "Sonya, Malachy, Fionnuala, and I play music. We have ever since I can remember, since childhood days. As adults, we've all had lonely stretches in our lives, and the music sustains us during these times, and reunites a bond when we're back together. It doesn't happen very often that we're all back at the same time."

"What do you play?"

"Lots of traditional instruments, but mainly Fionnuala plays the fiddle, I play the guitar and bodhrán, and Malachy plays the most haunting flute and tin whistle you're ever likely to hear. He sings as well. Actually, we all sing."

"You sing Malachy? That's lovely. I've heard Fionnuala already. I'm not surprised that you sing also, your voice is beautifully musical." He said nothing.

"So, you'll come to the pub?" asked Tim.

"Yes, I'd love to. You're all playing in the pub?" It had only just dawned on her properly. She was not usually this slow to catch on.

Malachy answered, "yes. It's a tradition that when the three of us are home, we'll play on a Saturday night. It started way back in Fionnuala's University days and kept on. No one asks us, it's just expected. It's one of the village's long-standing traditions. The three of us aren't home to-gether as much these days as we used to be, so there'll be a big turnout."

"And you can handle the crowds?" Tim needed her reassurance.

"Yeah."

"Not sure I can. I want you with a yearning I never knew was humanly possible." Malachy's face told of his earnest feelings, frank, despite the presence of his priestly mate, his mate he had in truth kept little from all his life. They knew each other's hopes and dreams deeply. They understood each other's fears too, and had lived the restricted, circumspect lives of valued priests.

Sonya sat with her arm dangling over Malachy's shoulder, pulling gently at his wavy hair. "What was the second question?" Both men squirmed, each wanting the other to start.

"Yes, well."

"Yes, well what? What's the big deal?"

Taking the plunge, Malachy said, "Sonya, would you come to church on Sunday please? I always take mass with Tim when I'm home, it's another little village tradition." He paused. "This one may be especially meaningful to me, and to Tim, and I guess to Fionnuala. It would be to the village too, if they only knew. It may be one of the last masses I say here. I'd like you to be there. It would be symbolic."

"But I'm not even Catholic."

"Holy Mary, Mother of God, Malachy! You didn't tell me that one."

"It slipped me, can you believe it?" He couldn't read Malachy's face now.

"This is madness!" Suddenly, Tim was outraged.

Now it was Sonya's turn to get defensive. Her religious background was not going to stand in the way of her chance for romance. "Madness, is it?"

"Very complicated. It'll be hard enough for Malachy to leave the church, but to get involved with a woman who is not a Catholic will be viewed as insanity, indeed, sheer and utter madness. It'll be viewed as a man whose lust has driven him truly bonkers."

"Surely you exaggerate."

"Sonya, I don't mean to put you down, or be patronising, but if you think I'm exaggerating, then you don't appreciate the power and influence of the church on the people's lives here in rural, coastal Ireland. It might have changed in the city, but it's not changed much in these villages. The younger ones who've left home to study or work might have changed, but the older generation hold firm beliefs on what is or isn't right, good, and proper. Perception and belief are intertwined."

"Can you keep quiet about not being Catholic?" Malachy was stalling. He didn't know what else to suggest and he wanted to appease both his mate and the woman he desired.

"Keep quiet about what?"

"About not being a Catholic."

"Would you mind awfully Sonya; it might make it easier for the moment at least?" Stalling seemed like a sensible idea to Tim also.

"I can manage that." She was not an atheist, but her religiosity wasn't a strong part of her life. Spirituality was though. Hers was more a sense of being in tune with nature and the Creator and a mystical power that brought colour and harmony in union. She believed in God and a supernatural power, and she remembered some Bible verses from her childhood days. The irony of Malachy's background was not lost on her.

"Good, so you'll come to church?"

"Why is it so important?"

"Everyone in the village goes, particularly when both Tim and I are present. The pub on Saturday, church on Sunday, village rituals. You'll get to realise that soon. If you are to be truly accepted in the village, you must be seen at church. And I've explained that it might be my last service that I take in the village, and thus I'd like you to witness it." On a more jovial note, he added, "besides, that way I can invite you home with Tim for Sunday lunch, and it would just look like Fionnuala is welcoming the new parishioner."

"Which is the real reason?"

"Let's leave it at that, shall we?" he replied with a twinkle in his eye.

One glance down to the ocean and Tim cried out, "Malachy, if we're not off now, we'll be trudging the long way around the road, or worse still, be caught in the tides."

"Just one minute to say goodbye properly."

"No, I've seen you Malachy, and I'm not sure you'd know what a one-minute farewell would look like, or in your instance taste like."

Tim waved goodbye and pulled his mate's arm. Sonya had to be content with a quick kiss as Malachy called over his shoulder, "be ready on Saturday night by eight o'clock."

Thoughts of the pub and of church mixed in Sonya's mind. Malachy the ordinary pub man, playing music to his local villagers, and Malachy the man of God, a priest saying the mass. The combinations did not make sense to her. Surely you could be one, but not the other.

Could she fall in love with a priest man? It was not right, was it? Or was it a matter of time?

Twelve

The next few days passed slowly for Sonya. She exercised her legs as much as she could and tried to paint, but mainly she spent time sitting around thinking about the romantic situation she had found herself in. She hadn't willed it; it had just happened. She reflected on how many of the good things in life happen this way, but just as quickly, she realised that so too did many of the bad things. You take and you put back, you gain, and you lose. Life's circles.

After the accident, she'd never thought she would want any man in her life if she couldn't have Malcolm. When she came to the village, she did imagine that she could hide away, and have minimal contact with other human beings. She realised now that this idea was stupid.

By nature, she was an out-going person. Being by herself had made her insular, so turned in on herself that she'd lost many of her normal social skills, particularly those appropriate for dealing with conflict and disagreement with others. She should have taken up the offers of counsel after the accident, but instead, she'd hidden herself away, quite incapable of dealing with the intensity of her grief. Consequently, too often, she was more irritable than normal. She hated herself for snapping at people, especially Malachy.

Being with Malachy had reminded herself how sociable she used to be. Everything in her life was dated, according to whether it was pre-accident or post-accident. Now, she was starting to categorise things whether they were pre-Malachy or post-Malachy. She realised that she must be moving on, just a little bit.

Thinking of Malachy stirred her, but it also troubled her. It was like taking something forbidden with one hand and having to put it back with the other hand. It made her think of a luxurious box of exclusive, hand-made chocolates, tempting her to take one more, then one more, and just one more, because she could. Oh, they were luscious! She could almost taste the rich, melting sweet swirling around her mouth, and with this sensation, she could feel Malachy's lips, more luscious than the most expensive chocolate ever could be. In a swift flash, someone whisked the box of chocolates away out of her reach, out of temptation. Who did that? Was it Fionnuala?

The girls in the hairdressers were right. Malachy was totally gorgeous to look at. It didn't seem fair that nature had blessed this man so richly with looks when no woman could enjoy them. His vocation ensured that the sort of desire she was thinking about was totally forbidden. He seemed oblivious to his looks, he'd clearly trained himself to ignore the passing admiration. Perhaps he no longer noticed them. Sonya had seen the nurses in the hospital cast more than a chance glance his way. He obviously took the attention as a trivial fact of life, no different from brushing his teeth.

Sonya tried to be honest with her feelings. She found him unbearably sexy but knew that these feelings weren't the same as being in love. She was enjoying the emotions of being stirred erotically, but like Malachy's sister, she was concerned with the speed at which Malachy was going to leave the priesthood for her. She knew that he'd not put it that way if he was sitting there beside her at this moment. He would say that he'd decided to leave anyway, and that she arrived onto the scene shortly after this. Three days in fact. That was quick! That was too quick! His was a forbidden love!

Time was moving on. In a few weeks, Fionnuala would be off chasing political stories somewhere exotic or dangerous. They would lose their chaperone and hardly ever be able to see each other. It was hard to decipher any sensible way around this dilemma. Then Malachy would have to go back to the seminary to give his superiors his final decision. Is he staying, or is he leaving? Will he change his mind after his superiors persuade him of his sinful folly? Surely what he was contemplating was recklessness.

Her mind drifted to all sorts of nonsense. She began to think about marriage. Then she kicked herself. What on earth was she doing? She couldn't believe she was thinking this. She told Malachy that three months isn't enough in anyone's life to make such an important decision as he was making. It was scary. Slowing everything down, seemed the only alternative to the helter-skelter of passion they were hurling on. She'd never liked speed.

She would resist his haste. She wouldn't give in a day too early. She couldn't be sure she was ready to say yes to anything, let alone in the fullest way possible, but when the time came, he would no longer be a priest, he would no longer be Father Malachy O'Sullivan, he'd be ordinary Mr Michael O'Sullivan. It still sounded a sexy name. She loved the ring to it.

As time crept by without seeing his lovely face or hearing his musical voice, she missed him. Without fighting it, she admitted it. She would have to get the phone put on but felt reluctant to do so. Something was holding her back, something mysterious that she couldn't work out. Whatever it was, it ensured that she was reluctant, hesitant, and tentative in her approach to this remarkable man.

Saturday night came. She'd spent the whole day preparing, having a long soaking perfume bath, one leg in an oversized plastic bag dangling over the edge, washing her hair, and preparing herself for going out with her man to the pub. It would be a novel night, a totally different experience for her, and no doubt, for him. But he was not "her man", was he? That was the whole point. This was frustrating. He was the local priest home on a visit. A priest is not a man in the sense she was thinking of, not a man who a woman could desire in the fullest sense. She must keep reminding herself of this.

His was a forbidden love. It seemed too much to cope with. This messiness was not what she wanted. The trouble was, every time she thought it wasn't worth bothering about, she saw his face in her mind's eye, remembered the feel of his body warmth, and in vivid fantasy, tasted his lips all over her body, reaching into crevices, curves, and openings that had been shut to any man for too long. These images were too arousing to ignore.

She took a last glance at herself in the mirror. She wore tight cream jeans, with one half of the seam let out to flap over her plaster, and a lemon buttoned shirt that she had tied jauntily at her waist. She had a lemon polka dot camisole top under her shirt, which let her undo a lot of buttons. The light colours showed off her blonde hair nicely.

"Sonya, my lovely one," and Malachy ducked inside for a brief kiss, "how are we going to do this tonight?"

"We will. It's lovely to see you Malachy. I've missed you."

"Have you really?"

"Yes."

"I'm glad. Let me look at you, my lemon blossom, you're adorable."

A long, impatient car horn could be heard, and Malachy piled Sonya into the back of the car with Fionnuala and got back into the driver's seat beside Tim. "Ready for tonight, Sonya?"

"I hope so."

Everyone was in lively form, chatting, laughing, and being light-hearted. It reminded Sonya of student days, when piles of her peers would squash into someone's car and go racing off to wherever anyone was racing off to. She hadn't been out socially since the death of her husband and children. Even when the children were young, she hadn't socialised much. Malcolm, being considerably older than she was, had preferred quiet nights reading indoors, so this boisterous playfulness was an intriguing experience. She liked it. It made one forget the cares of the world and enter the fun of the moment.

They arrived at the pub, walked in as a group, and Tim brought drinks back. Fionnuala, with grit determination on her face, plonked Sonya down beside Tim, and sat down herself beside Malachy. Then Sonya had to face multiple introductions. She had met quite a lot of people in the months she'd lived in the village, indeed, she even remembered many names, but knew little about them. Many of the women who had passed through the hairdresser's salon were here tonight, and she tried to be warm to them without disclosing much about herself.

The pub was full. From babies to grandparents, everyone was out tonight for a Saturday night get together and to hear the familiar, oh-so-loved traditional music. At frequent intervals, Malachy and Sonya passed knowing looks across the table. To be so close, yet so far, was a vexation. The cramped nature of the pub meant that anyone passing anywhere was pushed up close to whoever they were passing. Young people took advantage of this physical closeness. There were lots of friendly pats and hugs, more daring hands wandered over fleshy bottoms, and arms were thrown carelessly around bodies pushing past other bodies, but Sonya didn't move. She didn't want to be caught having to push past Malachy. She trusted neither herself nor him. Their arms would be compelled to entwine, and that gesture would be sheer stupidity. She was dreading her three new friends getting up on that stage. That would leave her having to fend for herself.

Just once, Malachy leaned across to her, placing one hand on her shoulder briefly as a friend might do, and said, "Everything okay?"

"Everything is fine."

He was not feeling so confident. His bright, bubbly personality meant that many people came across to their table to greet him heartily. He was well-liked. Indeed, he was loved, with a permissible love. Sonya was glad of the diversions and enjoyed watching his masterful handling of all sorts of people. As she watched the teenagers, the young men, the pretty women, and the older wrinkled farmers come across and chat, Sonya couldn't but wonder if he could give this all up, just for her.

For a few seconds, there was a break in the crowds hovering around him. "Are you really prepared to give all this up?" Sonya mumbled to him.

"Give up what?"

"Give up? Malachy give up the drink? Never!"

"Sh, Tim, I'm talking private."

"This is no place for private talk." His face said it all.

Ignoring him, she continued. "Sh, Malachy, how could you give all this up?"

Malachy was perplexed. He had no idea what Sonya was talking about. He repeated, "give up what?"

"You give this up, never," said Tim persistently, knowing the direction that Sonya was taking the conversation, and wanting to redirect it back to impersonal territory.

A natural distraction arose. A sophisticated woman walked by who Sonya had never seen before. "Josie, how are you?" and Malachy beamed and clasped the lady's hand, and she smiled suggestively at him, and moved on.

"Bit overly familiar, aren't we?"

"Sonya, there's no place for tight jealousy here. It's my job as a priest to be friendly to everyone. I don't discriminate. I show the same warmth to the beautiful people as I do to the less attractive ones. We've all got beauty inside."

Sonya wondered whether it was possible for any man to be totally objective and utterly good-spirited. "So, you're a priest tonight, are you?"

His exasperation was obvious. "You know what I mean."

This is never going to work Sonya thought to herself. Aloud, she repeated the question, "how could you give this all up?"

Tim interrupted jovially again. "Give this up? Never! It's his life."

Not sure what he was referring to, Sonya muttered, "that's my fear."

"Come on, Malachy, it's time we were playing." Fionnuala stood behind him, and, wrapping her arms around her brother's neck, placed her chin on his head. They looked lovely together, their jet wavy hair falling into each other, quite alike, and remarkably peaceful. Sonya looked wistfully away.

The music was wonderful. Fionnuala put all her energy into the fiddle playing. Her body swayed to and fro, speaking as expressively as her music. Tim was a master on the guitar, his fingers travelled up and down the strings with pace. He looked around the room, drawing on people's pleasure, and his happy face was a delight to observe. He and

Fionnuala had such rapport with their singing, they knew when to sing together and when each should go solo.

Malachy played the tin whistle and the flute hauntingly beautiful, just as Tim had promised. There was a pensive look on his face, as though he was being transported to spiritual realms. He didn't look at the crowds, he was lost in a magical world, deep in his inner soul. Sonya sat back, alone for the moment, watching Malachy fully absorbed with the sounds of the music. She saw people move across to her table, and not wanting to be rude, but also not wanting her focus to be interrupted, she stood up. Besides, she couldn't see Malachy as clearly as she wanted to from this seat. She walked across to the bar, perched on a stool, and ordered another drink.

Dermot Doherty was a typical Irish publican, cheery, affable, and a constant talker. "Wouldn't think they were priests, now, would you?" Dermot asked Sonya, jolting her out of her concentration.

"Oh, I don't know. Why not?" she asked casually, not liking the drift of the conversation.

"Well, have a look at Father O'Reilly playing the guitar like he was in a pop group."

"Can't priests be in pop groups?" she asked with a smile.

"Oh no, no, no," says Dermot, shocked at the suggestion. Would Americans never learn the ways of the Irish people he thought to himself.

Sonya turned back on Dermot, wanting nothing but to be left in peace to listen to the evocative music reeling through her mind. Whatever Dermot was thinking, it wasn't pop music that they were playing, but magical, Irish, traditional folk music. It pierced the soul, deep within. Sitting on a bar stool, she had a perfect spot to watch Malachy's face as the speed of the music changed, and they played some Irish jigs. Young and old were up dancing, and she was glad of the excuse of her broken leg not to be joining in.

"Father O'Sullivan now, what do you think of him?" enquired the continually chatty Dermot as he cleared dirty glasses, poured pints, and kept returning to her.

"Grand, yes, he's just grand," commented Sonya, evasively, deliberately using the colloquial sayings.

"Come on, you're American, you're a woman of the world, what do you really think of our Father O'Sullivan?"

"I'm not sure what being American has got to do with at all, but yes, he's grand."

"Isn't he just the most handsome priest you've ever seen?"

"Mm," she agreed, pretending innocence.

Dermot poured more glasses, then came to whisper conspiratorially, "I've heard what the young lasses say about him."

As she didn't want to hear what the young lasses say about him, she turned away. Perhaps she did want to know what they said. She could guess anyway. Was it any different from what she'd heard in the hairdressers? "What do they say?" she asked out of reluctant politeness.

She never got to hear the answer because the pub suddenly went quiet. Malachy had been singing rousing, lively tunes that most people in the pub knew and could join in the choruses, clapping and cheering wildly at the end. Suddenly there was a still hush. Malachy had raised his hand to the audience in an almost godlike stature. He paused and made an announcement. "I've got a new song to sing that you won't have heard before."

"Did you write it your good self?" a voice with a thick brogue called out from the back.

"Sure enough, I did. It's a song for every man who has known love but hasn't been able to enjoy his love."

Sonya caught the heavily disguised, troubled looks that passed quickly between Tim and Fionnuala. This clearly was unplanned, unwanted. Sonya felt herself trembling. She was glad that the pub was full and that everyone looked as hot and sweaty as she did. Her face was flushed, even though she felt weak at the thought of what might be coming.

As if Malachy was looking at her out of the corner of his eyes, and waiting precisely until she was ready, still, and settled, he was lightly strumming Tim's guitar, building up the atmosphere in the pub. The crowd was uncannily quiet, waiting. For what they were waiting, no one knew.

Malachy looked around authoritatively at his expectant audience, smiled, gave Sonya a fleeting glance as his eyes swept over the room, and said again, "a song for every man who's known love, but isn't able to enjoy this love. A song from a man who suffers the pain of a forbidden, unfulfilled love. Perhaps the story of some of you tonight."

Out of the mouth of Father Malachy O'Sullivan, came the most beautiful words Sonya had ever heard in a song. The song told of a man who was so deeply in love that the love was like a heartache. The words sung out the agony of separation for every second of the day that this man was away from his beloved. It told of the exquisite delight of being entranced by the love of a woman, and a voice that cries for the piercing pain of unconsummated desire. Malachy sung this song like a man possessed, there was no other way to express it, he was like a man in love.

There was a poignant hush in the room, even the children were quiet, everyone was captured by the moment. On its completion, he dared not look at anyone. He handed Tim his guitar, and, with a look to no one, and disregarding the wild claps and stomps, he pushed past people, and left by the front door. Everyone's eyes were on Malachy rushing out in haste. The claps stopped in unison, there was a moment of quiet, then the pub erupted into frenetic conversation.

The woman who had cut Sonya's hair, came over to her, and said, "well I never, can you believe a song like that?"

"It was lovely, wasn't it?" replied Sonya, trying to be evasive.

"Can you believe it?" stammered Fionnuala, who with one arm around Sonya, rescued her, called out her drinks order to Dermot above the crowd, and pulled Sonya across to a table away from the masses. They watched Tim grab a mineral water, and escape from people's clutches to burst out the front door himself, presumably in search of his mate.

"Why? Why did he sing that song, after everything we'd discussed and agreed to?"

"The man is crazy. He's normally so careful, controlled, in command. He's not himself."

"Hold on Fionnuala, what are you saying?" Sonya was annoyed with the implications of Fionnuala's remarks. "Are you saying that there's something wrong with him being in love, that it's a sign that he's going mad?"

"He's not himself Sonya, that's for sure. If he was, he'd have kept the song for tomorrow's lunch, just for the four of us and no more, or preferably, to sing as a lullaby to you, rather than broadcasting his love to the whole world." She was cross.

"He wasn't doing that. He was simply singing of the forbidden love of some unknown man for his woman, a love he can't realise."

"Yeah, yeah, Sonya, cut the naive romance, he may as well of sung, 'Sonya, I love you'."

"Sh, keep your voice down."

"Oh, worried about yourself, but not him. Ha!" Fionnuala was furious with Sonya, as well as with her brother. It was crucial to protect her brother's fine reputation. Maybe she was even more livid with Sonya for being the reason why she was upset with her brother. She was too annoyed to work out this subtlety.

"You know that's not true. I'm going out to find him."

"Don't you dare, you don't need to, Tim's gone out to find him," hissed Fionnuala, angry mother, prowling lioness, fierce house mistress, and bossy policewoman, all in one.

Sonya shivered in instant submission.

Thirteen

The pub conversation was distracted by crowds of individuals, couples, friends, and family groups, tripping over to their table to ask Fionnuala for explanations of the song. Comments kept swirling past Sonya's ears.

"That song isn't his usual style, is it?" asked the village mechanic.

"How can Father O'Sullivan know so much about love to write a song like that?" asked the old, faithful church organist.

"Reckon you'd have to know something about love yourself to sing as if your life depended on it," commented a young newly married woman, pushing her heavily pregnant bulk past them.

"Is Father O'Sullivan himself at the moment?" asked the principal of the village primary school.

"Where is he?" asked countless people as they moved past.

Fionnuala the journalist was highly articulate, as clever with the spoken word as the written word. She joked a witty remark to every comment or question and was glad of the interruption from Dermot who was calling her back to the stage. The problem was that her fellow musicians were nowhere to be seen. Fortunately, at this moment, Tim came inside, looking flummoxed, and whispered to Fionnuala, "he can't come in yet."

"What? Why ever not?" she asked, angry, frustrated, fuming.

"Says he can't handle it."

"That's fine for him to disappear. What does he expect us to say to everyone? People are asking awkward questions."

"He wants us to say that he is praying for the man in the song."

Fionnuala sat back in disbelief and uneasiness, then broke out into a relieved, raucous, stress-busting laughter. "I'll give it to him, that is very clever! What an ingenious brother I have, that'll get them talking more, wondering who the heck the poor man is, but it will surely take the weight off his own heavy shoulders. I like it," she laughed long and heartily, in some release of the enormous tension that had built up inside of her.

Tim and Fionnuala went back on the little makeshift stage, and Tim made the announcement with a very serious look on his face. "Friends, Father O'Sullivan will be back shortly. He's spending some time now in prayer for the man he knows who is in love, but the woman has rejected his love, and thus he is in total despair. This man has asked Father Malachy to pray for him, and that's exactly what he is doing right now."

Cries went up, as people crossed themselves religiously, "ah God bless him."

"Dear Malachy, what a kind man he is. We're so lucky to have him as one of our priests."

"Oh, dear love the man, God bless our beloved priest."

With that last comment, Tim and Fionnuala broke out into lively reels, and sure enough, the crowd forgot the suspense and began some wild dancing. Sonya wanted dearly to go in search of Malachy. She didn't want to be the cause of his pain. She missed him now, even while he was out of this room, but couldn't bring herself to tell him, for fear that what she was feeling, wasn't true love, and that in raising his hopes, she'd hurt him in the long run.

After some time, Malachy wandered innocently back, and with congratulatory pats on his shoulders, and handshakes as he came back in, he stepped into his spot and joined in the music. Few in the crowded room would have noticed the glare Fionnuala gave him. It was brief. Tim grinned his usual cheery grin. Malachy looked down at the ground, not searching for Sonya's face.

The night ended. Cries of "give us a finale, Father O'Sullivan, give us the love song again," could be heard all over the pub.

"Yes Malachy, give us the love song again," came the chorus from young and old.

But Malachy wouldn't be tempted. He made it clear to his fellow musicians that he wanted to leave as soon as possible. The car was parked down the lane a bit, and there was no one outside with them when they packed their instruments away. Malachy threw Tim the keys and jumped in the back with Sonya.

"Steady, Malachy, you've already made a fool of yourself tonight."

Hearing the intensity of anger in her voice, Tim interrupted, "now now, it's all right. The little story about the man in love needing prayer worked its tricks."

"So, we ridicule prayer now, do we?" queried Fionnuala, a religious woman herself, unusually furious with her brother.

"No. We don't ridicule prayer. The story wasn't entirely a trick. Indeed, how much truth do you want? It's just that the man was me, obvious to us four and no more. I was outside praying for guidance." He paused. "And would you believe it, for self-control? I didn't find it an easy night. I need to be here with Sonya now. I need to feel her body beside me. You heard my song. I can't do without her. You might not like what you hear, but I tell the truth, tough as it is."

Tim and Sonya wished for a thoughtful space for silence, but Fionnuala was totally stressed out. "Malachy what made you sing that song tonight? Why couldn't it have waited?"

"Didn't you like it?"

"Malachy don't be infuriating. It was a beautiful song but singing such a love song made it very hard for all of us. I couldn't believe that you'd do such a stupid thing."

"I am a man in love Fionnuala, get used to it."

"You're just being ridiculous." Anger he'd never heard in her voice hovered heavily.

Ignoring her fury, Malachy sat cuddling Sonya, their fingers entwined tightly, knowing that it was too dark on these windy roads for a passer-by to see. As they came close to Sonya's house, Malachy said to his sister, "I want five minutes."

"You can't."

"I can and I must."

"This is madness Malachy. People will drive past, see Tim and I in the car, put two and two together, and by tomorrow, word will have got around that Father O'Sullivan who sings love songs, was in kissing the American woman with the luscious curls."

"They'll not see anything, and all I'm doing is helping Sonya to the door."

"It will be fine," reassured Tim, not rebuffed by her irate glare, "I'll get out too, that will make it seem reasonable."

Inside the door, Malachy was unusually quiet. They stood looking at each other, dark eyes holding blue eyes in a powerful hold. "Tonight, was a profound night for me Sonya, my darling."

"The song was so beautiful; I could have cried."

"Did you?"

"There weren't many dry eyes around me. Of course, my eyes were wet, but I had to disguise it. When did you write the song?"

"I had the tune floating around in my head for a while. On the first day, when I hadn't seen you, I sat down and started playing with the words. I was missing you intensely and was cross with you for not having a phone. There were many times when I wanted to pick up the phone and speak to you, and hear your voice. I was missing you sorely, and the words just flowed. Contrary to what Fionnuala might think, I didn't know that I was going to sing the song tonight. I saw you there and couldn't resist it. I acted on a whim, which as Fionnuala knows, is totally uncharacteristic for me. Part of her anger lies in being unaccustomed to seeing me respond to an impulse. As a priest, I must be constantly orderly and forever self-controlled in every space of my life. There's no space as a priest for whim or risk. Tonight, I had to sing the song. Something deep inside me compelled it. I guess I didn't think through the consequences properly. I saw it as a love poem. Fionnuala thought it was too explicit and inappropriate for me as a priest."

"They were beautiful words Malachy. Now, you must go."

"You're beautiful, Sonya." He waited, hoping she would say something meaningful, but she looked away. Not understanding herself, bewilderment mounted. An impatient car horn tooted. Malachy kissed her lightly on the cheek, and with a "look forward to seeing you tomorrow," he shut the door and was away.

Sonya went straight to her bedroom and lay on her bed. To love, to be forbidden to love, to desire, but not to know whether this was love, was tangled. Would it unravel in time?

She wasn't looking forward to the morning. To watch Malachy in the church, ministering the faith with Tim, would surely highlight all the erect barriers that she saw to be vivid in their relationship, barriers that couldn't easily crumble.

Her last thought before she fell asleep was to wonder why romance is excruciatingly complicated.

Fourteen

The memory of Malachy's song, the love poem as he called it, transported Sonya in her dreams. Floating in soft clouds, she saw figures in the background playing music. They were almost angelic figures holding minute musical instruments. These figures were a blur, they merged with the powdery softness of the clouds drifting by. There was only one person who stood out clearly, her Malachy. Her Malachy? Was that how she thought of him? The song was a love poem for her. Bafflement reigned. She floated away in the softness of the sleepy cloud.

To say that Sonya was nervous on Sunday morning when she woke was an understatement. To be present in church watching Malachy and Tim would be painful to say the least. It was fine for Malachy to think that this might be his last occasion saying mass in his local village, and that it was important to him that she was there, but she was the reason that it might be his last.

Guilt overwhelmed her. He would dispute any need for guilt and say that he'd decided to leave his vocation regardless of meeting her. But it wasn't easy for Sonya to view it that way. She felt that she was to blame for the enormous disruptions that were to happen in Malachy's life. That sense of personal responsibility was hard to come to grips with. And at this stage of the relationship, she wasn't sure that she was going to fall in love with him, certainly not in the speed that Malachy would like, if at all. Everything about this relationship was new to her, a new man, a priest, a man who was forbidden to love. Guilt refused to leave her.

She knew also that she was starting to cause Fionnuala trouble. The closer it got to the time when Malachy would have to give his final decision to the church, the more Fionnuala would resent Sonya, or so she thought. She was relieved to know that Fionnuala would have returned to work by this time. But then she and Malachy would lose their guardian angel, and their contact alone together would have to be limited. Then today, there would be doubtless comments from the churchgoers about the love song from last night, and Sonya would have to smile politely and offer courteous comments in reply. How could she do it?

Not wanting to stand out too much this morning, she chose a plain outfit from her wardrobe. It was a simple long-sleeve pastel pink and sky-blue check shirt dress which she buttoned all the way up, then feeling too formal, she undid the last two buttons. She pulled on a conservative pink cardigan. She was dressed and ready far too early. That's always a mistake, she thought, because all you do then is pace up and down feeling increasingly nervous, fixing your hair again, looking in the mirror, and panicking. She tied her hair back and loosened a few curls. At the exact agreed time, a car horn tooted, and Tim came to the door to greet her. Malachy, in the driver's seat, smiled his greeting as if she was any old parishioner they were collecting.

Sonya reverted to her insensitive old self and snapped, "putting a clerical collar on changes you, does it Malachy?"

Fionnuala flung her a fierce lock. "Leave off Sonya, this isn't an easy day for Malachy, or any of us for that matter."

Sonya sat back quietly furious with herself. Approaching the day entirely from her own point of view, wanting Malachy's lovely face to smile at her, wanting his musical voice to greet her, longing for his strong arms to be flung about her, was a terrible reflection of her selfish streak. "Sorry," she said to everyone. "You look very dignified in your church collar." She chose the words carefully. He just smiled, seemingly incapable of speech. Sensing a change in his demeanour, she asked him, "are you nervous, Malachy?"

"Yes, strangely I am. The same words, the same actions, the same chants that I've said diligently and repeatedly all my adult life, words that I could say backwards in my sleep, and now, I'm suddenly afraid I'll forget them, stumble over them, or confuse them."

"Is that because I'll be there?"

"Don't be so horribly conceited," Fionnuala replied crossly. "It's because it may be his last time. The church has been his life Sonya, it is his life Sonya, get a grasp on that, hold it firmly before your eyes, and see what it might be like to let go of something you've held onto so dearly for most of your life." She was already grieving for his loss.

Sonya suspected there had been fierce exchanges between brother and sister this morning. She knew she would have been at the centre of them. Not wanting to cause this sort of strife, she was overwhelmed by feelings of personal culpability. This sort of inner agony wasn't fair on good, kind, loving, lovable Malachy. She didn't love him. She would have to tell him this before it was too late. Hoping to redeem herself, she said, "it might not be your last mass Malachy."

Fionnuala, an exasperated look over her face, could only ask, "what on earth do you mean now?"

"Malachy can stay in the church and forget me."

Tim, ever quick to harmonise and prevent any conflict, and not wanting his best friend to be upset before this potentially momentous occasion, just said, "let's have the service now, and this discussion over lunch. Peace be with you both."

He was right as usual, and they drove the rest of the journey in silence, everyone lost in their respective thoughts. The two men hastily alighted from the car and went away to the back of the church to get changed into their robes. Sonya went to apologise to Fionnuala who she knew was inwardly raging at her. The tension wasn't worth it. She didn't want to be the cause of a broken relationship between a brother and a sister, and she didn't want to be responsible for such a cataclysmic change in Malachy's life. She would break the relationship now before any more heartache was caused, before Malachy made his drastic decision.

She entered the church cautiously, feeling like she was a stranger to the social world again, as if the coming out process she had begun had ended instantly with her decision to walk away. All she wanted to do was to withdraw back into her little safe hole and escape from the peering crowds again. She began to quiver. Fionnuala didn't hold a grudge for long. Without knowing the specific details, she sensed a little of what Sonya was going through and held her hand briefly to calm her.

Tim and Malachy walked out together, resplendent in their flowing white gowns with purple and gold satin trimmings. Malachy looked exceptionally impressive, but a bit terrifying also. This was Malachy the priest, not Malachy the man. Whether he liked to admit it or not, Sonya couldn't help but distinguish between the two. They presented different identities with different lives, expectations that knew little overlap.

Despite his fears, he didn't confuse any of the well-rehearsed lines. Without doubt, he gave a command performance, like the true professional he was.

Watching him disturbed Sonya. This was not the man who had lifted her aching body, soothed her brow, held her in his arms, and kissed her. Indeed, this wasn't even the man who, in the pub last night, had sung the most beautiful love song anyone had ever heard.

This was Malachy the priest, not Malachy the man. The two identities were different, and she feared that Malachy the man, would always be ultimately, Malachy the priest. It was a good thing she'd come to church and seen him like this. Now she knew that she couldn't lead him on any further. Just as it was with Malachy, today, was a momentous day for her too. She would have to tell him that he should stay in the church because she couldn't continue a romantic relationship with him. She would be direct and straight. He would be under no false pretences. Fionnuala would be relieved. Her escape would be back to her hidey-hole where she would bury herself away again, shelter, and paint.

After church, she shook hands with Tim and with Malachy as if she was no different from anyone else. In her mind, she already was no different. Malachy gazed into her blue eyes, searching for some sign of compassion, but saw none. He was saddened. Sonya stood around with Fionnuala as they were greeted by all sorts of people. Around her, she heard congratulatory comments about how wonderful Malachy had been that morning, as if he was inspired by God.

It was a quiet foursome that drove back to the cottage. The tensions of the morning, the pressures of the service, and the wariness that hovered over what was to come, left everyone drained. On reaching the cottage, Fionnuala went straight into the kitchen. Tim opened a bottle of wine and lit the fire. Malachy pulled Sonya to him and led her down to his study.

She hadn't been in his study before. It was a simple, plain, masculine room, befitting a priest. He went to hold her, but she pulled back. "Sonya, please, I need you."

"No Malachy, it's not me you need, it's the church."

"Oh Sonya, come here, don't resist me."

"No Malachy, it's not to be."

"Sonya, my lovely one, don't do this to me. I've been pining to hold you in my arms again, to hold you close."

"No Malachy, it won't work." Her stubbornness dominated. There was a harshness in her voice.

There was desperation in Malachy's voice as with some frustration clear in his tone, he asked, "what won't work?"

"Your love."

"Sonya, don't tell me what will and what won't work for me." There was a discernible strain in his voice. "I know what I want and what will work for me. I love you."

"But I don't love you."

The words stung like a bullet. They were harsh, metallic, brutal words, aimed at killing the spirit. He had been shot. But Malachy's response was, as always, loving. Although saddened, he said some surprising words, "don't hate yourself, Sonya."

Now this was not the response she had expected. She wished that she wasn't so blunt or abrupt with her remarks. Her fiery temper wasn't her friend. He was again having to respond to her cruel harshness with his caring humility. "What do you mean?" she asked more aggressively than she meant. "I don't hate myself."

"No, but you put up barriers to stop people getting close to you. Let yourself be happy Sonya and, let me show you happiness again. Don't spurn my love, for I love you."

She changed the topic. "Malachy, I found it strange to watch you in church today. Too strange for words."

"Try to explain it. What do you mean?"

"I found you magnificent and yet formidable."

"Why formidable? What do you mean?"

"I don't know, it's like as if in putting on your full priestly regalia, you become unapproachable. The robes signify that you are the church's representative. This makes you unapproachable to someone like me. Malachy, you're a priest, not a man in love with a woman. The church and you are one."

"Oh my God, Sonya." His impatience mounted. "You refuse to heed what I say to you. Don't you think I know at first-hand, my romantic feelings? Don't you think I know exactly what the church thinks of that?" Apart from the phone saga, this was the first time he'd been cross with her. She saw it in his face and heard it in his voice. "There is a major communication gap between us!" His fingers tightened into a fist, and he pummelled his palm. Nervous energy and an overabundance of adrenaline needed its physical release. He was struggling.

"Maybe it's impossible to cross that gap. I think that's what I'm saying."

"It's just not true. Well, it doesn't have to be true. You constantly create barriers. You erect them yourself. You want me, you communicate this desire to me, then bail out," and his fist pummelled his palm furiously, "you withdraw, every time." He fell silent for a while. "I found it strange to have you there in church today, but I was glad you were there. To have you so near, yet so far, to have to pretend to the world that you are no more than the next pretty woman in the pews is a personal form of hell." Malachy was leaning on his study desk, and went to sit on it, trying to pull Sonya to him. She resisted. His face was the picture of sadness.

"I can't, Malachy."

"You can't what?" There was a new tone in his voice.

"I just can't."

"You can, but you won't."

"That's what you want to think, Malachy."

"And what you want to think, is that I'm making my decision about the church based on some silly whim, like singing the song last night, or like falling for your gorgeous curls." Even Sonya smiled briefly at this crazy suggestion. "Yes Sonya, mine is an enormous decision, but I have made it. I am leaving the church. If you want to cause me hurt by not letting yourself fall in love with me, then I guess there's not much more than I can say to persuade you. But please respect my decision, that's the least you can do. I am leaving the priesthood, and I do love you."

Fionnuala's voice could be heard calling them to lunch. Neither wanted to leave the study with so much left unsaid, but neither knew what to say quickly. Malachy's arms tightened around Sonya. It was impossible for her to resist, but this time he sensed her physical reluctance. She lay comforted for a tiny moment, then pushed him aside.

Her stubborn streak was dominating. She repeated, "it won't work."

"It can." His eyes held her, magnificent eyes, kind, deep, tantalising in intensity and in their expression of love. She resisted his visual seduction.

She was either cruel or crazy, or perhaps both. Or maybe grief for her first husband stood as a barrier to new love.

She was a widow; he was a priest.

Fifteen

Everyone seemed to need light relief, and surprisingly, lunch was a pleasant, happy affair. The wine flowed freely, loosening the tongue as well as the spirit. Only Malachy was a little on edge. Every time he looked across at Sonya and saw her face, skin as soft as a ripe peach, eyes as blue as the summer sky, hair shiny blonde as the sun shining on a sea goddess, his eyes melted. He was growing more and more in love with this woman who seemed to be growing further and further away from him. Sonya avoided his eyes. She was relieved to have Fionnuala back in their company as happy and gay as ever, and Tim was always placid and fun.

After lunch, she helped them clear away, in her limited, hobbling capacity. Malachy had disappeared. They sat by the fire, the unspoken question of Malachy's absence hovering.

On his return, Tim joked, "disappearing has become your specialty, has it?"

"Ha ha," he said, strangely not amused.

He went to perch on Sonya's seat, but Fionnuala interrupted this. "You can't sit there Malachy. This lounge is open for all and sundry to see."

"Come and sit on the sofa with me then Sonya."

She shook her refusal. Tim saw the hurt look in his mate's eyes, and trying to be light-hearted, jokingly put his arms around Fionnuala whom he considered almost as a sister. "Make a foursome, shall we?"

Fionnuala pushed him aside, energetically, with great mirth. "Glad I know you well enough to know that you're joking Father O'Reilly." Tim went strangely quiet. He knew that if his situation in life had been different, if he hadn't been called to this noble profession, this was certainly the woman who he would have wanted for his wife. They would have been a great match. He sensed that she knew it too. He wished the Church hierarchy would change their views.

Malachy went to stand up as if he was leaving the room again. Tim, missing nothing, leapt out of his seat, drew the curtains, and with a firm hand on his childhood mate's shoulder, and with a knowing look to his long-time friend, said, "you two desperately need to talk. Come Fionnuala, we'll go off for a short walk, grab your jacket, the wind has picked up."

Fionnuala, unable to resist it, called over her shoulders a needed reminder, "behave yourselves," only to have a friendly hand clasped over her mouth.

Both man and woman sat, space between them, sad, like lost people, their anchor adrift. "Sonya darling, this is stupid."

"No more stupid than our situation. It won't work Malachy, it's too difficult."

"Nothing that's worthwhile is too difficult."

"I'm not sure that this is worthwhile. It will ruin you."

"Listen to my words, I don't know how many times I have to say them, but I'll repeat them as many times as I need to say them, to convince you. I love you. I am leaving the church. This is a momentous decision to make, but it is sad that the church doesn't let men in love stay. That's a fact of life. Perhaps in years to come it might change. I have made up my mind. I'm not equivocating or indecisive. Furthermore, and importantly to me, I am very much at peace with myself and with God. I am quite certain about what I am doing. I am equally certain that I love you."

"I'm not certain, Malachy." Again, her words were too quick. They didn't give time for reflection on Malachy's explanations. They hastily hurtled through the room, knocking any careful sensitive clarifications aside, and crashing them heartlessly into useless crumbs.

Malachy came across to her, and knelt by her feet, clutching onto her dress. "Sonya, my darling, I can't live without you." He spoke slowly, hoping that the words would sink in.

She ruffled his luxurious jet hair and pushed him away. "Go back Malachy, little sister said so. You've crossed the safety barrier."

Instead of smiling, he simply said, "forget my sister's bossiness. I want to hold you, be near you, and show you how much I love you. I can't stand the pain of separation. I need you so badly. My ache is a physical, spiritual, and emotional need, that I never knew could be this intense."

"Malachy, I don't need you in that same sense. I've known love. I need my peace now. I want to be by myself." Even as she said the words, she didn't believe them. She wasn't sure what made her say that.

"Sonya, I don't want to tell you what you do or don't need, but I don't think you want to be by yourself any longer. We talked about that in the hospital. You've come through that stage; your life is in transition. It needs to keep moving. Make a space in it for me, please. You're a warm, lovely person, who melts at my touch."

"Other times I'm an icicle, am I?" she asked mischievously.

"A bit frosty, but I'll match you with my love, and believe me, you will melt," and he crept along the floor like a polar bear about to leap, relieved at the positive change in atmosphere, when he was startled by a tap on the window.

Peering out of the window at a small space where the curtains didn't meet, he saw an older woman tapping frantically on the windowpane. "Oh my God," he whispered to Sonya.

"Who is that?" she hissed.

"Mrs Althorp, resident village gossip," and he arose, walking to the door, the man converted back to the priest.

"Hello, Father O'Sullivan."

"And what can I do for you, Mrs Althorp?" With no invitation, she stepped inside.

"Well, it's slightly delicate," and she nodded in the direction of Sonya.

"Anything that needs saying, can be said here." His face was resolute.

"Didn't know you had a visitor, Father."

"Just being hospitable, Mrs Althorp."

"Fionnuala around, is she?"

"Out for a brief walk with Father O'Reilly, they'll be back soon. My visitor can't walk far. Now what did you want to see me about?"

"Can I have a private word with you, Father?"

"You know I don't have private words on a Sunday unless they're urgent."

At this, Mrs Althorp was stumped. "Then I'll be back tomorrow, Father. A good day to you, Mrs Painter," she said smugly, a nasty smirk on her face.

"Oh no, I just don't believe it," Malachy said as she drove off. He dumped himself heavily into an armchair. "She might have seen me crawl across the floor. Wait until my sister gets home, she'll hit the roof."

Sonya responded in typical extreme fashion. "And that's why I can't be seen with you again. I'm breaking off any relationship we may have been forming. I won't be the cause of your good reputation being lost."

"No, no, no, my love. You don't have to be this extreme." His face reflected the desperation he was feeling, an ugly sick churning feeling in the depths of his stomach.

"It might be extreme, but it's necessary. I have to do it."

"No, Sonya, don't do this to me. I need you. I want you. I can't live without you. Don't cut me off." Desperation was in his voice.

The back door banged and in walked two flustered beings. "It's starting to drizzle. Don't tell me it's true? Whose car did we see drive off?"

"I'm afraid so. It is true. It was exactly who you feared it might be."

"This is my nightmare come true."

"Not only yours Fionnuala, but this is also a shared nightmare. Malachy my friend, no matter how much you're in love, you can't do anything that might harm your fine reputation, or ours for that matter."

"I'm not."

"Yes, but it's going to look like that. You were sitting away from each other, weren't you?"

Both Malachy and Sonya looked across at each other, then looked at the ground. Malachy stared into the fire. "Of course," he said unconvincingly.

"Malachy, what were you doing when Mrs Althorp knocked on the door? Tell us precisely." This woman's voice expressed the fact that she wouldn't be meddled with. She demanded a straight answer.

"To tell you the truth," he began sheepishly, "I was crawling across the room toward Sonya. I hadn't quite reached her."

"I don't believe this. Are you mad? Don't you know that she'll be spreading vicious rumours to everyone she meets. The phone will be running hot. Malachy, you've lost any good sense you may have had."

"She couldn't have seen much through the curtain. Tell her I was looking for something. Tell her Sonya lost an earring, and she couldn't get down on the ground with her broken leg, and I was trying to find it. That's a feasible explanation."

"That sounds plausible," Tim remarked, relieved at a simple way out of the dilemma.

"This stupidity has got to stop. You're reduced to inventing crazy pathetic stories about men in love in need of prayer, and women with sore legs who lose earrings. It's ridiculous! It's madness! I've had it! It's got to stop!" Her voice was unusually high pitched.

"It will stop."

"What do you mean?"

With a tenacious look on her face, Sonya sat up stiffly in her chair. "This has been a peculiar day for me. I wasn't sure how I'd react to seeing Malachy in the church." She was glad of the presence of Tim and Fionnuala, but she addressed her speech entirely to Malachy. "Malachy, my dear," the words were not lost on Malachy, Sonya hadn't spoken so dearly to him ever before. She realised this too, smiled, looked embarrassed, and stared into the fire.

"Do you want us to leave?" Tim said quietly.

Fionnuala interrupted him speedily. "We're not going anywhere."

"No, it's fine, please stay. Malachy, you looked wonderful this morning in your robes. You are so commanding, excitingly masculine, yet your religious fervour was obvious. I know your story, I've tried to let it sink in, but it won't. Until I know I can return your love, and I don't know if I ever can...." Her voice trembled and broke off.

"Sonya?" Malachy's voice was appealing, he anticipated what was to come, and he didn't want to hear it. The pain screamed out inside him.

"Until I know that I can return your love, I won't do anything that will hurt all of you, because in this Fionnuala is right, you are all implicated. I've grown very fond of the three of you, and I am immensely grateful to you for helping me to recapture the fun in life these last weeks. I won't ruin your reputations. Malachy, the relationship can't continue. You'll have to stay away from me."

Malachy knew from the firmness in her voice that there was no point in arguing. "You will get the phone on, won't you?" It was a question that had only one right answer.

"Yes."

"Thank God for that."

"It will take time Malachy; you know how long anything official like that takes out here in the coastal wilds." Fionnuala's realism was not what Malachy wanted to hear at this moment. He looked pathetically sad, totally forlorn, like a puppy pulled prematurely away from his mother's tit.

"Come Sonya, I'll take you home," Tim said, knowing that Malachy needed space to work through this difficult stage in his life.

Malachy arose, and went across to Sonya, but Sonya stood up quickly and turned her face away from him. "Please Sonya, give me a kiss goodbye."

"I can't Malachy, it's goodbye."

Quietly, but firmly, he replied "it's not goodbye, it's nothing as final as that, it's just, see you later."

"Perhaps."

She didn't look behind her, or wave as they drove off. She remained steely-faced the entire journey. There was not a scrap of emotion on her face. When the car stopped, Tim, in his typical wisdom, said, "cry Sonya, go inside and cry. Be honest with yourself. Admit how much you are falling in love with Malachy."

"I'm not."

Ignoring her, he continued, "maybe you are. Think on it. You'll certainly miss him. Admit that to yourself at least. For God's sake, get the paperwork about your phone done tomorrow, don't delay that. Fionnuala is right, the process takes ages out here. He will need some contact with you. Poor man!"

"I'm not sure than any contact is sensible."

"Sonya!" Tim was exasperated. He was starting to sound like Fionnuala.

"Goodbye, and thanks for everything," she said as he helped her to the door, and she left him looking disappointed.

Sure enough, the second she'd closed the door on the outside world, she burst out crying, speaking aloud, "what have I done? What have I done? Malachy, I want you. Why can't I have you? Malachy, Malachy." The beautiful sound of his sexy name circled through the air, but this time, it sounded hollow. There was nothing in it. Malachy was no longer part of her life. She had seen to that. She had thrown him out, tossed him aside.

She walked into her bedroom and feeling no emotion about what she was about to do, she lifted the photo of Malcolm off the wall, kissed it lovingly, and lay it face down on the floor beside her bedside table.

Sixteen

Sonya woke up the next morning in a state of shock. She had said goodbye to Malachy, she really had. He was no longer part of her life. Despite this self-imposed void, every conversation she had ever had with Malachy, every look that had passed between them, raced around in her head. Reliving these special moments was a paradox. The recollections were agonisingly painful, and yet they brought excruciating pleasure. Pain and pleasure, pleasure and pain, intertwined in a jumbled mess, which is exactly what her life seemed to be.

A life without Malachy was unthinkable, but surely, she didn't love him. How could he become part of her life then? What was love anyway, she asked herself? Didn't she have strong feelings toward him? Didn't she quiver in thrill every time he touched her? Didn't she crave his touch like nothing on earth? Wasn't that enough?

Deep down in the innermost depths of her being, she knew it wasn't enough for a man who'd devoted his entire life to God and to the church. Nothing but her total devotion would be enough. Until she could give him this promise of complete faithfulness, she would be compelled to stay away from him. But maybe she could never offer him a total commitment, and then what? Was she doomed to a life of misery, always to be alone? Was she to be a lone painter, wondering what she was losing out on? She had come to this village wanting to be alone, small comfort now.

Moments blurred into days, sad days into lonely nights, restless nights into troubled days, and Sonya moved like a ghost around her house. The cottage that she loved dearly for its warmth and cosiness, suddenly seemed cold and void of human life. She was running into the danger of hiding herself away, again. Like a scared mouse running back into her little hole, she was escaping from people, and from the life outside of her door. Now, she didn't care. Nothing seemed to matter. She sensed the dangers of a retreat to old bad habits. Her rediscovered social skills would be lost, she'd become withdrawn, and lose all the sparkle for life again.

Looking for a diversion to her melancholic pining, she tried to paint, but her inspiration had vanished. The beauty of the colours still excited her, but beauty reminded her of Malachy, handsome, desirable Malachy, no longer part of her life. She had struck him out. He hadn't left by choice. Of that, she was in no doubt. Her miserable lot was entirely her own fault. There was no one else to blame. The knowledge made her wince. How crazy was it to throw away the possibility of romance, the seductive excitement about sensual touch, and the possibility of knowing the fulfilment of love? Love frightened her, as did the prospect of the loss of love, and the absence of love.

Every morning when she got up, she almost tripped over the photo of Malcolm that she'd removed from the wall. Not once did it occur to her to place it back. Something else was happening in her life now. It was time to move forward. But she was shuffling backwards.

At last, her plaster cast was off. Seamus had cheerfully collected her to take her to hospitable for the grand removal of the plaster. She was a little more mobile. However, she remained in her cottage, not venturing outside, and not having contact with a single other person.

Dymphna's car pulled up one day, and while she knew that it was horrifically rude of her, she didn't answer the door. The warm cheeriness of the kind doctor's wife would have made her feel too lonely when she left. She sensed that Seamus knew a little of Malachy's feelings toward her, and Sonya wasn't emotionally ready to have to explain details of her present life to Dymphna. Occasionally, she felt neurotic, whatever that meant. She wasn't crazy.

One day, she sat in the garden for a whole afternoon, watching the road, irrationally hoping to see Malachy's car and a glimpse of the driver, no matter how brief the sighting might be. There was little traffic passing. There had been a few locals that she'd recognised drive past, and some tourists, but no Malachy. Feeling stupid, and freezing cold, she ran herself a hot bath. The steam faded the strain momentarily.

Everything was easing along satisfactorily until she realised that she was quite out of food. It was a long walk into the village. Before the accident, she would have enjoyed the walk without a problem. While her progress was excellent, she wasn't back to full strength yet. Feeling confident that she could manage to drive, she went out to the garage, but the car that had sat untouched for a long stretch now and during harsh weather, unsurprisingly refused to start.

"Damn," she said to her car, uncharacteristically kicking it roughly with her good leg. "If the phone was connected, I could pick it up and have a mechanic come out." But she hadn't signed the forms that were necessary to have the phone connected, even though mysteriously, yet not entirely without surprise, the appropriate forms had arrived through her letterbox one morning. They had not contained a letter, and the address had been typewritten, giving no clues as to their source. The postmark was smudged. She guessed that either Tim or Malachy had sent them, dear men that they were. Or, perhaps it was practical Fionnuala, yes that was most likely.

Now, needing a lift into town, all she could do was to stand beside the road and hope that a car would come along soon. Wasn't that what a small village was about, helping each other out? Thinking about this made her annoyed. "You knew how much food I had Fionnuala, why didn't you come and help me?" She wasn't being fair. Fionnuala had helped her out wonderfully, and she'd hurt Fionnuala without apologising. She'd caused messy conflict between a brother and a sister, and she hadn't been empathetic.

Waiting for a car to pick her up made her irritable. For some weird reason that she couldn't articulate, she hoped that any passing car would not belong to Malachy. She hoped even more that it would not be Mrs Althorp. Now if it was Tim, that would be nice. Tim was safe and predictable. He was a great comfort, but a cheery person also.

Rugged up, she waited for forty minutes before a car sidled up beside her. "Need a lift?" a friendly voice asked.

"Thanks so much Dermot, I've been waiting for ages and I'm getting cold, I'd be so grateful for a lift," and she piled in, happy that it was with someone she felt comfortable.

"Haven't seen you around much lately."

Quick as a flash she responded, "I've been resting my leg."

Looking down and seeing the plaster off, he asked, "isn't it better yet?"

"Nearly."

"Then you'll be back in the pub this week. It's Fionnuala's last Saturday before she's away again, so there'll be another grand session of lively music. Wonder what treats Father O'Sullivan has in store for us this time?" and he cast her a piercing look.

Innocently, she simply replied, "I wonder."

"Not sure that he can better the love song though, aye what?"

"Not sure myself."

"So, we'll be seeing ye, will we?"

"Who knows?" Inwardly, she was seething. Why hadn't she been asked already? How does time pass so quickly? Was Fionnuala going back so soon? Had something changed to make her leave earlier? Had Malachy changed any of his plans? But did any of these matters concern her at all? Hadn't she chosen to cast these wonderful people out of her life?

"Where shall I drop you, Sonya?"

"Anywhere is fine, I just need some groceries," she said absentmindedly.

"How will you get home?"

"The bus comes along soon enough." The bus was erratic and unreliable, she knew it, and so did Dermot. She didn't care.

She was relieved to be dropped off. Her mind was full of mixed and stressful thoughts, and she had a lot to do. First, she posted her letter requesting the phone connection. She knew it would take a long time for the paperwork to be finalised and for technical engineers to come out. But it was a gesture of her intention that she was going to reconnect with humanity again.

Next, she had to find a mechanic. That took time. She should have asked Dermot for his advice. One person sent her off in one direction, the next person sent her off in another direction. Eventually, she found someone appropriate, but in typical Irish fashion, he wasn't going to be rushed. "Sure, I'll be out soon enough," didn't seem like a commitment.

Next, she had a long list of groceries to buy. She was tired at the mere thought. Her heart pounded and raced as she saw Malachy's familiar car parked in the market square. She looked around quickly, but there was no one on the street. A cold wind was blowing. Anyone with sense was indoors. In the supermarket, the first person she literally bumped her trolley into was Mrs Althorp.

"Mrs Painter, we haven't seen you for a long time."

"No," she answered curtly.

"Haven't seen you since I saw you up at Father O'Sullivan's house." A snooping look smeared her wrinkled face.

"Visiting Fionnuala I was Mrs Althorp, and if you'd excuse me, I have a lot to do."

"Doesn't have to pretend she's so high and mighty, does she now?" Sonya heard her complaining loudly to the shopkeeper who quite rightly chose to ignore her.

Sonya didn't care about this gossiping woman's rudeness, she simply wanted to do her shopping in peace, and to be on that bus as quickly as she could. A small part of her wanted desperately to see Malachy, the bigger part of her couldn't bear to see him. She wasn't sure which was the most accurate part.

Struggling out of the shop with a full basket and bags in her other hand, a fierce wind whipped by. She wished that she had her car to dump her purchases in. The wind was icy. A biting chill ripped across the market square, blowing her hair wildly across her face. She almost stumbled and tripped, so she didn't see who was standing in front of her as she tried in vain to push her hair out of her face.

A welcome hand grasped her arm and took her basket out of her hand. "Sonya, oh Sonya," she heard a whisper and nearly gasped out loud. The familiarity of that sexy voice, deep and husky, with such a musical lilt to it, raced through her, exciting every bit of her body. She shivered with the cold outside, and with the flame burning inside.

"Malachy, how lovely to see you." Her delight was evident, and it thrilled him.

"Have you missed me?" he whispered.

"I've not wanted to admit it." Sonya was rapidly looking around to see if anyone was overhearing the conversation.

"But have you missed me?"

"I've tried to live by myself, as if I don't need anyone else."

"It doesn't work, does it?" She smiled in half assent. "Come, it's freezing. Where is your coat?"

"I didn't realise it was going to be this cold."

"Get used to it. This time of the year can be fiercely cold. Go nowhere without your coat. Come and have a cup of coffee with us?"

"Us?"

"Fionnuala and me."

"Is she talking to me?"

"Of course, she is. It was you who said that you weren't going to see us, don't you remember? We've kept away from you, respecting your wishes."

There was no need for Sonya to feel awkward with Fionnuala and Malachy, but she did. Fionnuala greeted her warmly. She was abundantly nice. "Hey, how are you? We planned to call in to see you this afternoon." She made her announcement in a loud voice, as if to the whole coffee shop.

"Truly?" she asked in a hushed tone, partly in wonder, in disbelief, and hope.

"Oh yes," said Fionnuala, detecting Sonya's confused vibes, and understanding a little of what she was going through. Her heart went out to this woman who, despite trying to persuade her brother to the contrary, preoccupied his every waking moment, and she presumed, much of his dream time.

The steaming coffee warmed Sonya, but not as much as Malachy's presence. He was quiet, observing Sonya and Fionnuala chatting. It was such a simple joy just to be sitting at the same table as the woman he loved with a longing that grew daily, despite her absence from him, and despite her rapid tendency to lash out.

"So, what's this I hear about you returning sooner than expected?"

"How do you know about that?"

"Small village, remember? You can't keep secrets from too many." Her eyes sparkled. "Dermot gave me a lift into town. He told me."

"Yes, I'm cutting my break short, just a few days sure, and I can take these days some other time."

"Perhaps for a wedding," Malachy whispered.

His comment was not appreciated. "Malachy, don't," said Sonya annoyed, hastily looking around her.

"Malachy, don't be stupid," said Fionnuala, disgusted, refusing to take him seriously.

"Sorry," he said with a grin, not bothered by the reactions of his two favourite women in the world.

"I had a phone call from a friend of mine who wants me to go on a fact-finding mission to a remote part of South America on the border between Argentina and Chile. We're going to a part of the mountains I've never been to before. I can't resist this trip. I've always wanted to go. It will be a marvellous experience."

"Speaking of phone calls, did you apply for your connection Sonya?"

"Can't we keep this just to a general discussion of life?"

"Asking about phones is quite general, Fionnuala." It was his turn to be unusually annoyed. "If Sonya had the phone connected, she could have called us for a lift into town, and you could have rung her to let her know you were leaving. Have you sent the forms off?"

Sonya asked, "what forms?

"Don't tease me. I can't stand it. Have you?"

"Did you send them to me?"

"It doesn't matter who sent them. Have you sent them off?" His voice was desperate, he was drowning and wanting a life-support, or at least wanting to know that a lifejacket could be thrown his way shortly.

She smiled. "Yes, today." The relief on Malachy's face was a picture.

"Can we give you a lift home?"

"Yes, and please stay for dinner?"

"We can't." The disappointment on Malachy's face would make anyone cry. "We have people coming over late afternoon for dinner. I'd invite you too, but I don't think you'd enjoy their company. Mrs Althorp is one of them." Fionnuala grimaced at the thought.

"She was nagging me in the shop."

"Don't let it worry you, although it's easier said than done."

They piled the groceries into the car and drove off. Everyone was notably coy as they stepped inside with parcels under their arms, uncertain of where to take up conversation, what could or shouldn't be assumed. Atypically, it was Fionnuala who appeared the most restless, walking up and down like a caged lioness. She was frustrated with her brother's intentions toward this woman. They had had so many arguments these last weeks over Sonya, the priesthood, and what Fionnuala believed was the mistake her brother was making. She wanted to flee. Work gave her an escape route.

Yet she was an intelligent, sensitive woman. What struck her forcibly, was that through every disagreement and argument, her brother's position did not falter. Not once was there a flicker of change in his story, not once did the story meander, or deviate to the left or to the right. It was the same story every time. In many ways, this consistency reassured her, at the same time, it aggravated her. She knew his story by memory, and it revolved around and around in her head. It was as if the more times she went over it, the easier it would be to finally accept it.

He kept reassuring his sister that he'd spent four years pondering and praying about how to cope with the lack of intimacy in his life. His respected mentor Father Paddy Ryan had discussed it in depth with him, indeed it was he who'd intuited it, and had raised the issue. Because he thought it genuine, Paddy had given him three months of official leave to make a definite decision. Was his life to revolve around the church or a woman?

Malachy had told his sister that he'd decided immediately into his leave that no matter how hard the break with the church would be, it was the love of a woman he craved. At that point, he didn't know who that woman was. Three days into the break, he knew with a surprising but absolute certainty that he was falling in love with Sonya, the beautiful, much pained American woman who he knew nothing about. His story didn't waver.

Knowing him well enough to know that he wouldn't be doing anything major in his life without a lot of prayer, contemplation, and reflection, Fionnuala knew that ultimately, she had to respect his feelings as well as his decisions. It was thus with grit determination on her face that she turned to the disheartened couple standing before her and said, "it's too cold for me to go out walking or I would. I've got some letters I need to write. I'm going into the conservatory to write them. I'll give you thirty minutes to talk, and not interrupt you. Go and unfold the secrets of your heart, then I have to get home to prepare food for guests."

The widow and the priest smiled at each other.

Seventeen

Grateful to Fionnuala, they sat rather formally on the opposite ends of the sofa. They were lost in separate worlds, unsure of how to meet halfway.

"We shouldn't waste time," begun Malachy, and he slid down the sofa nearer to Sonya.

She held up her hand like a bossy traffic warden. "No Malachy, no further."

"Why Sonya, why do you hold back on me? You seemed pleased to see me out in the market square today, struggling with your full basket, and your beautiful hair blowing wild and free. I saw the delight on your face, and that thrilled me. Your hair is the only part of you that you occasionally allow to be wild and free." He paused to smile before turning serious again. "I'm finding life very difficult now."

"And I'm to blame?"

"I'm not looking to blame anyone. Fionnuala and I are at each other's throats for the first time in our lives. I know she was incredibly relieved to have the phone call from a journalist friend, and an excuse to escape to exotic places."

"She resents me a little, doesn't she?"

"You could be anyone."

"Thanks for the compliment."

"Oh Sonya, don't be so over-sensitive." He reached across and twirled a ringlet within his fingers. This time, she didn't pull away. "What I meant was that Fionnuala would be jealous, angry, and upset, all those emotions, with whoever I'd fallen in love. That woman is you."

"Jealous?" Sonya asked. The thought had never crossed her mind. Angry and upset yes, but never jealous. "How is she jealous?"

"Come on, that's not hard to understand. We've been the most important person in each other's lives for twenty years. That's a long stretch for the sort of closeness we share. Remember, she was ten, I was fourteen when we were left orphans, with only each other to love. I'm thirty-four now, and she's thirty. For twenty amazing years, we've nurtured each other. We've been together in all our difficult times. She's encouraged me through my lonely patches when the church wasn't giving me everything I needed. I've sustained her through broken love affair after broken love affair. She can't seem to find the man of her dreams who'll make her happy." He looked away, thoughtful, as if he knew who that man might have been.

"Go on Malachy." Oh, the joy of saying his name again, it brought unspeakable bliss. She had to admit it, not that she was going to tell him.

"Well, it's a curious idea, but as an explanation, the other night I sat in the rocking chair in her room, and that's where I thought about it."

"Her room? What were you doing there?"

"I wanted to be reminded of you. She was out visiting friends. Sitting in the rocking chair by the window, I could picture you lying there tossing to and fro, muttering restlessly in pain, and eventually calming."

"Did you do that often?"

"Every day you were there. I spent every waking moment that I could in the room with you, praying, meditating, and falling in love with a woman whom I didn't know." He looked wistfully away, as if the mere word "love" caused too much pain to utter it out aloud.

"About your original point Malachy, did that have something to do with Fionnuala?"

"Yes, it did." He paused again. "My God Sonya, you're beautiful."

"The story?"

"Mm, the story." He kept going. "As I was saying, the other night as soon as Fionnuala left the house, I sat on the rocking chair. Immediately, I saw your image on her bed, but it wasn't the pained image with the bandage around the head, but my wife, naked and voluptuous, breasts pert, and sitting up in bed, waiting for me to ravish her." He spoke about this image as naturally as if it had been an acceptable part of all his life, not as if it was an image that was thoroughly inappropriate to a priest-man.

"Malachy, ought you to go on?"

As if that was a stupid question, he ignored it. "It suddenly occurred to me, that Fionnuala might have problems in relationships with men because of her closeness with me. It's possible that every time she draws nearer to a man, she thinks that this intimacy will mean she'll draw away from me, so she releases her bond to the man. That causes friction, and they breakup."

"Quite a psychoanalyst, aren't you?"

"It's part of the job these days."

"As a priest?"

"Yes Sonya," he said with a degree of force, "as a priest. It is part of my job to understand people's motives." He continued, "the conclusion I came to was interesting. It is that if I do marry, Fionnuala must accept that. Indeed, I've seen a shift in her these last few days. She's still angry, terribly cross, but I think that's because she's started to believe the reality of my love for you, and knows that despite fighting it, sometime soon, she should accept it. I think that when I marry, Fionnuala will be able to let herself fall freely and fully in love."

"So, you're doing her a favour?"

"Yes, unintentionally. It's a by-product of my love."

"That's very impressive, Malachy. You're very perceptive." She meant this as a compliment but was scared that it sounded cynical.

"It comes from hours and hours of giving counsel and advice to all sorts of people, from young couples in love, to newlyweds, to women who can't conceive, or women who have too many children, or who grieve over sad miscarriages, to single mums, often teenagers who've told no one else about their pregnancy, to men guilt-ridden by their illicit, messy affairs, to elderly farmers who can't survive on their miserly pensions."

"You're a very kind man Malachy, you really care about people, don't you?" There was no sarcasm in her voice.

"Yes, I do. When I go back to the seminary to inform Father Ryan of my tremendous decision, I have a specific request. I'll ask for a pastoral position in the church, a counselling job where the church sanctions a wife."

"You'll be very good at that."

"Counselling or having a wife?"

He wasn't in the mood to respond to this jest, so changed his tack. "Now, enough talk about me. How have you been? How are you honestly? It's great to see the plaster off. More importantly, have you missed me?"

"I don't know." She shrugged, trying to avoid facing up to the pain and the exquisite agony of love that she read vividly in his face.

"What do you mean you don't know? How can you not know?"

"I don't know."

"Have you missed me?" Malachy edged a little closer to Sonya, hoping that she wouldn't notice, and that she wouldn't brush him aside. Oh, how he yearned to be touching her. He knew that he had precious little time alone with her, and that with his sister leaving and going overseas, he'd have no further excuses to be alone with her. But he was aware that Sonya wasn't showing any signs of eagerness toward him. He would not force himself and be humiliated by rejection.

"I'm not even sure of my answer to that."

"Oh Sonya, why not? It's such a basic question, you know, or you don't know." There was frustration in his voice.

"I'm confused. I've gone back to hiding. I'm a mouse in my little hole, sometimes, I'm a scared rabbit in my burrow."

"You're neither a mouse nor a rabbit. Come to grips with it. Your whole personality has blossomed since you stopped hiding. You've come to life again. I'd like to think that I played an important role in helping you to find yourself."

"You did, Malachy." She reached out to hold his hand, and as with every time she touched him in the slightest way possible, she burst into a spirited vitality again. He was right about that. Malachy took the move as an invitation to hold her, and she lay back in his arms, content for the first time since she was in his arms last. What a difference he made to her life. Why would she not admit it to herself and to him?

After a while, Malachy, looking at his watch, conscious that his sister would be a rigorous timekeeper, turned his body to face her full on. Cradling her shapely face in his hands, he moved slowly toward her so that their mouths were almost touching, but not quite. He held this position briefly. Then he pulled back. He hoped that it stirred in her a knowledge that what you cannot have but earnestly desire, you often crave more than if it was handed to you on a silver platter. He knew that his action deprived himself, but hoped it was worth the effort.

"Sonya, I love you." His face was earnest.

"I know."

"Are you quite sure of that?"

"Yes."

"Sonya, I'm leaving the church. I wanted to go to tell Paddy earlier, but he forbade me. Formal rules of the church, making certain of massive decisions and the likes. But I am leaving. That leaves me free."

"Really?"

"Yes. Sonya, will you marry me?" His eyes were moist with heartfelt love, such a tenderness that it was impossible not to be deeply moved.

Sonya brushed her hand over her own damp eyes. "I can't Malachy."

"Why not?" She shook her head, not sure what to say, not sure what her real reasons were anyway.

Malachy knew that his time was up, that his sister would march in at any moment and break the warm-hearted atmosphere between them. He put his hand on her soft cheeks and, knowing that his touch stirred sensations in this woman, he kissed her hard on the mouth. She responded eagerly, their mouths searching for the answers to unanswered questions. "Sonya, I love you."

"I know Malachy, my dear." He smiled again as she spoke those rare but exceedingly tender words that he loved to hear. "I love being with you, but..."

"There will come a time when the 'buts' will disappear. I wait impatiently for that time." He voiced a confidence that he didn't always feel.

With the precision of a Swiss watchmaker, Fionnuala reappeared, Malachy sat back. Without a lot of tact, she plunged in right from the start. "Come Malachy, we must be off. Sonya, will you come to the pub for my farewell bash?"

"I don't think so."

"Please Sonya, you must come." Malachy's eyes sucked her in, they were tender, and spoke more than words could say.

"Don't worry, there won't be a repeat of last time, no more love songs from my dear daft brother."

"I can't."

"Please Sonya, you promised you wouldn't drift back to hide away. If you don't keep coming out and about, you will wander back, and then you'll retreat into your shell again. Whatever you finally decide about me, you live here now. You're going to need the friendship of the villagers. You should come out for that reason alone, as much as any more pressing reason like I'm desperate for any chance to see you."

"Malachy, the priestly counsellor," remarked Sonya, a trifle unkindly.

"The man with the forbidden love," joked his sister.

"Hence the song," he replied. "I'm still praying for that man. It is but a matter of time for him. Please say that you'll come. We'll pick you up at the same time."

"Yes, I'll come, but only if you promise no drama Malachy, no drama at all."

"No drama, my love, I'll keep my song for you only."

Fionnuala whisked Malachy away. Sonya walked around the room lost. She wandered into her sanctuary, but it no longer gave her peace. Photos of her dead husband, daughter, and son, were the memories from the past. Oh, they were very precious, but they didn't help her to redefine a new life.

At last, she knew that. Malachy was right in encouraging her to move on, and to avoid hiding again. She didn't want to hide repeatedly, but life without Malachy was not worth it. Was that why she'd been hiding these last days? Had she finally admitted to herself that she could not live without him?

Was it a matter of time before she gave in?

Eighteen

There had been too much tension around Sonya of late, and she was determined to go out for a Saturday night outing in as lively spirit as she could muster. It would be a fitting farewell to Fionnuala, and it would show Malachy a side of her personality that he'd not had the chance to get to know. She hadn't given him the opportunity to see the bright, bubbly side of her. The more she thought about it, the more she started to get excited about the evening out, and to be truthful, she was looking forward to being with people again.

In her youth, she'd been gregarious, particularly in her student days. They were lively, fun-filled days. Malcolm, loving as he was, had been quiet and restrained. It was only now that she was prepared to concede this fact. They hadn't gone out much, and certainly had never been out dancing. And with the children very young, she had been preoccupied with seeing to their happiness. Yes, she was going to have fun tonight. She even practised a little jig around the kitchen to test the strength of her leg. It was making good progress.

Dressing in bright colours made her feel high-spirited, so she carefully chose a bright red skirt with layers of material. When she spun around in a circle, the layers swirled around in front of her. Remembering how hot it became last time, she wore a plain white Vee-neck t-shirt, and pulled on a little red vest with silver sequins sewn in. Katie had loved their shine. The memory of this made her smile, and she realised that this was the first time something like this had happened, where her child's face had popped into her mind with a lovely reminder of the past, and she could smile rather than cry. That was nice. It was a gradual but real recovery of her emotions taking place.

Even though Malachy loved her hair flowing, she tied it back into a loose ponytail with a silk red scarf draping, and then pulled a few tendrils free to soften the looks. She wore big circular gold earrings, knowing that the whole gypsy affect made her look young and carefree. And that's exactly how she felt. It was an exciting sensation. Quite new. A red dash of striking lipstick finished her off. Her reflection in the mirror pleased her.

She pulled a long plain coat on so that no one would see the outfit until she arrived. However, there was to be no shield pulled over her mood. Tonight, was one to be free, easy, and totally relaxed. This was a night to be enjoyed to the full. That Malachy was to be a part of it was taken for granted.

When Tim came to the door to collect her, it was a different looking woman that stood there. He saw the easy-going change in her temperament immediately, and grinned, his enormous, infectious grin. What a delightful man he was! As had occurred last time, there was easy laughter, and loud shrieks of delight as the foursome sped off down the hill for a night in town. Sonya hadn't felt as young and as free since she was an art student. Yes, life could be good.

Everything was fine as they carried their musical equipment into the pub and Tim helped Sonya take her coat off. She could not help but be pleased to see Malachy's face. She certainly heard Fionnuala hiss under her breath, "goodness me Malachy, look elsewhere."

Malachy blew air slowly out of his mouth like a diver coming up for breath. Pushing past Sonya on his way to order first drinks, he sputtered lowly, "my gypsy princess."

Sonya loved it. Tonight, she was going to love everything. She almost looked mischievous. Fionnuala was on edge. "Careful, Sonya."

Raising her eyebrows heavenward, she copied her, "careful, Fionnuala. Tonight's the night to throw caution to the wind."

"Don't."

"I'm only having you on, cool down, my friend."

Drinks came as the foursome sat down, Sonya swinging her ponytail from side to side. Both men were accustomed to handling all sorts of situations so ignored the niggling between the two women. Or at least, Fionnuala interpreted Sonya's buoyancy as deliberate provocation and was worried. There was no need to be concerned. Sonya was merely being cheerful as she'd planned.

"The gypsy look, is it?"

"Whatever you like, Tim."

Sonya caught Malachy's look, a look that was bursting to say what he thought, and simultaneously, they exploded laughing. The mutual release was wonderful. Tim was pleased. It was okay in a pub. He leaned across to Fionnuala, that wonderful woman who he was so fond of, and said, "relax, they're happy, let them be. They're not doing anyone any harm."

"Aren't they?"

"Accept it Fionnuala, stop fighting it."

"I'm getting there," she said reluctantly, knowing that he'd understand exactly what she meant. Unable to remain in their presence, she grabbed her glass of Guinness and moved to another table.

Her space was quickly taken up by a group of youths. This meant that everyone had to change places and move around. With a subtle wink, Tim orchestrated the moves and made sure that Malachy had to be squashed up to Sonya in a way that would be acceptable in a full bar, but nowhere else in the village.

"Thank God for full bars," he yelled into their faces, as the noise level increased tremendously. He grinned and went off to join another table. It was sheer bliss for Sonya and Malachy to be sitting close, with thighs, calves, and shoulders touching. When Malachy leaned forward in animation, joking easily with the youths who he knew well, he pressed into her body even more. He leaned forward at regular intervals, maximising this opportunity to be pressed together. She could feel his muscles ripple as he moved forward and then back.

Sonya marvelled at the effortless rapport that Malachy had with these young people. It made her feel nostalgic for the students she'd taught over the past years. She had loved their enthusiasm, buoyancy, and bright attitudes to life. Maybe she and Malachy would make a good team, they could be youth leaders together. She would start a club and teach the art skills that she loved to practice. He would counsel disturbed, confused, and frightened youth. How ridiculous to even be thinking like this!

Attention turned to her, and she wasn't prepared for it. Rather shyly, one girl, with lovely red hair, asked, "are you living in the village with us?"

"Yes." She smiled.

"Do ya like it, missus?"

"Yes, I do."

"What do you do?"

"I paint." She wasn't familiar with the way of these young people, they were trying to be friendly, but she didn't want to be drawn in fully. With a hand on her thigh and carefully disguised under the table, Malachy rescued her, as usual, she was thinking.

Too soon, it was time for the musicians to take their place on the stage. With a firm knowing press into her thigh, Malachy was off to join the others. Sonya had made up her mind early in the evening to enjoy herself, and that she was going to do. The music started up with quick, lively dance tunes. It didn't take much for these Irish people to be up on their feet, pushing tables and bodies aside, tapping away, the cares of harsh lives thrust away for the night. Bodies were gliding, jigging, and stomping around the room. The young mixed comfortably with the old, ducking and weaving around their parents, aunts, uncles, and cousins, looking for any excuse to rub cheeks with newly found boyfriends and girlfriends. Some people danced with partners, others danced alone, except you were never quite alone. There was always someone right there beside you.

Across the bar, Sonya caught Dermot's eye and he chuckled cheerily. He winked, and surprised at her nodding assent, he came from behind the bar and pulled Sonya to her feet. He led her into the middle of the gyrating masses, and despite his unruly appearance and Guinness-girth, he was a smooth dancer. Sonya loved dancing, but it had usually been by herself or with Katie. She especially loved the thrill of the speed and the skill of moving sensuous bodies touching close to another. She threw herself back into dancing with every bit of enthusiasm her recovering leg would allow. Seamus grinned at her across the floor, delighted that his patient was up dancing carefully.

Most of the villagers lived a simple life. Few families had much spare cash. Times were hard, and they shared what little they had. People were dressed as smartly as they could afford to dress, but no one had the panache, glamour, and newfound sparkle of Sonya. Without trying, she stood out starkly. With her red skirt swishing in full around her bare legs, the dim lights catching the shine of her sequined vest, the blonde hair, loose and pretty in its red scarf swaying from one side to the next, she was the star attraction. Dermot kept steering her near the musicians, and she kept steering him away. He was more dominant, and she caught Malachy's eyes as she spun this way and that way in delight. Their eyes could say what their words could not.

Tonight, Malachy could watch this woman innocently. Every man in the room was doing so, as well as most of the women. The locals were astounded. It was like having a professional dancer in their midst. From being an uptight, withdrawn, grumpy woman, she'd been transformed into this free, gregarious, gay woman. She appeared totally uninhibited. Her sensual body flowed with the music. She looked beautiful, a wild, carefree gypsy woman, dancing to the beat of the music. It was a physical liberation.

Exhausted, she took a break, Dermot gave a passing kiss on her head, and she flung her arm confidently around Seamus. "You've done a great job on my leg, doc," she laughed.

"It's great to see you up dancing," said Dymphna, "though I'm not sure where you get your energy from." Dymphna was a trifle dumpy in appearance, plodding about in her own way.

"I've always loved to dance," she said, happy with life, relishing the night to the full.

The musicians took a break, and over her shoulder she saw Tim glide Malachy away from her. At the angle that she was sitting, she couldn't even see Malachy. How badly she wanted to. It wasn't that she was dancing for him, in fact tonight, she was dancing for her own enjoyment, to remind herself of the joys of sensuality again. But when she knew that men's eyes were on her, and what woman doesn't know this, tonight, hers was an exhibition of dancing for Malachy.

She wanted him to see her body in motion, close to another man who'd never be his rival, affable, lovable, over-weight Dermot the publican. She wanted Malachy to be excited, even if he needed to disguise it.

Impatient to be back dancing, she was glad when the second half of the music session began. Willing her on, the musicians played lively dance music. Several men she knew by sight pulled her up on the floor and wanted to dance with her. In jest, she pretended to dance with all three, weaving in between each one in turn. They were flattered with her attention. She hoped she wasn't showing off. Then suddenly, she became aware that she was showing off her body, but she no longer cared about feeling self-conscious. As she'd warned Fionnuala, it was a night to throw caution to the wind.

She wasn't flaunting her body in an inappropriate way. But she was undoubtedly relishing the delights of her body in motion. Every bend and twist and swing highlighted her neat waist, her feminine hips, her glorious breasts, and her stunning hair. She sought Malachy's eyes and smiled. She caught Tim's face, and he grinned his wonderful smile. How lovely for Malachy to have such a marvellous friend, she thought graciously.

Not unsurprisingly, she tired, her leg started to ache, and Seamus asked her to stop and rest. Cries of, "give us a song Father," could be heard. Malachy hadn't sung much tonight, keeping the dance tunes lively and continuous, keeping his eyes on Sonya's dancing. Tonight, he wouldn't be tempted to sing songs he ought not to sing. Temptations of other sorts were too strong. He ignored the cries circling the room.

He called the pub to a hush. Expectant faces waited for what was to come. After the previous occasion, anything might happen. Sonya felt a rush of excitement but saw the look of immediate concern on Tim and Fionnuala's faces.

"A song," he said, "a final song."

What would Malachy sing tonight?

Nineteen

Cries went up around the pub. "Give us your love song, Father," called the bus driver sitting at the front bar.

"No, tonight I'll sing 'the parting song,' a song in affection to my sister. Fionnuala, my dear sister, we all wish you well, and trust that God's richest blessings will be bestowed on your travels." He sang the traditional, well-known song in a heartfelt way, and everyone joined in the chorus, heartily singing.

> "Here's a health to the company, and one to my lass.
> Let's drink and be merry all out of one glass.
> Let's drink and be merry, or grief to refrain,
> for we may and might never all meet here again."

Malachy raised his glass, and called out, "a toast to my sister, safe journeys, and may God's blessing and protection be on you always, until we do meet again."

Cries of, "safe journeys," went up all around the bar. Fionnuala was touched, and she embraced her brother warmly. She moved around the room quickly, giving people hugs and kisses.

The four left as the crowds were already dispersing. As with the last time, Malachy went to sit in the back with Sonya, but this time, Fionnuala snatched the keys from him at the same time as he went to ask her. "Go on you two, have your last cuddle and kiss."

"Last for a while you mean."

Last one, what did they mean? Sonya wasn't sure, but let the warmth of his embrace reassure her, and in the back of the car, oblivious to their fellow passengers who were merrily chatting away, she snuggled up to Malachy and kissed him like a schoolgirl, hungry for his mouth, starved of his affection. She was in paradise. But there was a limit to where hands and mouths could go with a fellow priest and an authoritative sister sitting in the front of the car.

The car arrived at the cottage too soon. "When are you leaving, Fionnuala?" she asked.

"Tomorrow night."

"Tomorrow night? I didn't grasp it was that soon."

"Will you come to church tomorrow and back for lunch, my love?"

Sonya was pensive. "No, it's better for you two to have the last day home together."

"No Sonya, that's not so," Malachy rebutted, but Sonya had seen the look of relief on Fionnuala's face.

"Will you come in for coffee then?"

"Well, it must be a quick one. I still have some packing to do. It's important that we come in for a short time, you have to say goodbye to Malachy as well as to me."

"Goodbye to Malachy, what do you mean? Malachy, where are you going?" There was a mournful look of panic over her face.

"My love, I'm not going anywhere. It's just that with Fionnuala gone, Tim will be my last chance for a chaperone. Finding an excuse to be with you will be difficult." He stopped, "that's if you want to be with me. You keep changing your messages."

"Let's go inside, just for a short while," came Tim's suggestion, sensible as ever.

Sonya was thoughtful while she prepared the coffee and listened to Fionnuala. "You really had a ball tonight, Sonya, didn't you? You're a wonderful dancer. Everyone in the pub loved watching you, women as well as men. It gave Malachy a superb excuse to cast his eyes all over you." The men chuckled. "Everyone else's eyes were glued to you, so it was no different for him to be doing so. You're a fabulous dancer. You become the dance." Sonya beamed at Fionnuala.

"I hope I've not overdone it with my leg. Seamus warned me to slow down."

They chatted generally, and suddenly, Fionnuala bounced up business-like. "Sonya, come with me, I want to talk to you in private. Then Tim, you and I will shuffle away for a few moments while the lovers kiss and cuddle in peace." The men sat grinning. Sonya rose, uncertain of what was to come. Fionnuala took her into the kitchen and shut the door. They stood there, woman to woman.

"Well, Fionnuala, it's goodbye for now."

"Sonya, I'm going to cut to the chase. You've come into my life as an uninvited guest. I won't pretend it's otherwise. But I like you. You've got warmth, vigour, and life. I liked watching you tonight enormously. Like others, I got pleasure in seeing you swirl around the room and imagining the joy you could give my brother. We're women of the world, we know the delights of the flesh. I'm sure my brother has told you a little about the rows we've been having. I've come through most of them, reluctantly, I might add. At last, I am convinced that he knows what he's doing. I need to go away now and let it all drop into place in my stubborn head. I want you to know that I'm accepting of you now, even of the future role you may play in my brother's life."

"Thank-you." There was clear gratitude in her soft voice.

Ever business-like, she continued. "Now, I want to make a plea to you."

"A plea to do what?"

"Not to resist your love for Malachy. I don't believe you're the sort of woman to lead him on. I've seen you kissing him enough times to know that you do desire him. Don't cause pain in dragging out your resistance."

"I'm not doing it deliberately."

"But you keep giving him mixed messages." Fionnuala's face was flushed as the frustration she often felt with Sonya mounted. "You go hot and cold on him in a flash. That's not fair. What's he supposed to think of your changes in attitude and mood toward him? You kiss and then you reject him the next second."

"I know it's not fair." This was a massive confession.

"Get clear with your feelings, Sonya and communicate them clearly. Admit to yourself that you miss him, that you want him, love him, and will marry him, and make him happy forever. Now, will you?"

"I can't promise you all of that."

"Promise me you'll think about it."

"Yes."

"Promise me that you'll do more than think about it. It's not fair to confuse Malachy. He is the best man alive, Tim aside." She was quiet, presumably thinking of both men. Sonya wondered if she did love Tim a bit, and if some of her anger at Sonya was her deflected frustrated desire toward knowing she could never have Tim as anything other than a dear friend, almost a second brother. Neither women could dwell on this possibility. "Promise me, Sonya."

"Yes, I will."

"Then come and say goodbye. Who knows, I may be your sister-in-law one day." The women clung on to each other in a warm embrace, signalling their new relationship.

"Take care, Fionnuala."

They went back to the men. Fionnuala called out to Tim, "come, my man."

"In your dreams, my woman."

"In your nightmares," she quipped laughing, masking any emotion that might have been in her yearning.

"Sonya my dearest, come to me. Time is short." Malachy kissed her swiftly. "I'll write to you. I'll type the letters, so my writing isn't detected. Perhaps we can arrange to meet on the beach. I'll give you a day and a time when we can meet. Your leg is strong enough to take the steps down to the beach, now, isn't it? Will you meet me?"

She nodded and kissed him. "Malachy, I miss you when I don't see you regularly." Rapidly, she mentally noted that she'd fulfilled the first part of her promise to Fionnuala.

"I know, my dearest. These next thirty days will be the biggest trial of my life. Living without you, biding time for a decision I have already made seems like nonsense."

"Kiss me, Malachy."

"With pleasure, my darling." Their lips caressed while their bodies screamed unfulfilled desires. He tasted the salty, dance-induced sweat on her neck, and wondered about the taste on her belly, breasts, thighs, and higher up, spaces he was quite ignorant about. Wanting to explore forbidden territory, he resisted. Voices came toward them.

Innocently, Tim did not so much as glance in their direction, always the proper priest and gentleman. He called out, "take care Sonya, see you around."

"Don't forget my hopes for you, Sonya," called Fionnuala as she walked out of the door, not looking their way.

"My God, you're adorable. If this is a taste of what's to come..." He couldn't finish. In eager, innocent delight, his look was boyish. "Sonya my love, I hope we bump into each other in the village. Please write to me, otherwise I'll arrange to meet you at the beach. Until then, know that I love you." With that, Malachy was gone.

Thirty days, how was she to cope with not seeing him for that long? She had admitted she missed him. What was the next stage? Admitting she wanted him? Oh yes, she could do that easily, her body screeched its desire to be one with him.

Did she love him? Not yet, or was it more than she would admit to herself? Perhaps it was just a matter of time.

Twenty

The last thing Sonya did that night before she lay down to go to sleep, was to lift the photo of Malcolm off the ground and put it away in a bottom drawer. It was a symbolic gesture that she was ready for the future, whatever it might bring. She then knelt by her bed, something she hadn't done since she was a child, and prayed, "God, please help me."

She slept restlessly, a childhood rhyme revolving through her head. All she could remember about the rhyme was, "thirty days hath September, April, June, and November." The word "thirty" kept leaping out to mock her. A leprechaun, dressed in green with shiny horns and the number thirty stuck on horns in luminous colours was in the forefront of her brain. She woke with a start. "Thirty", why was the word tormenting her? But of course, that was the stretch of time she had to go before Malachy was a free man, no longer a priest-man, but a man who could declare his love not only to her, but to the rest of the world.

Her instinct was to reach for the phone. She had always had a phone beside her bed. She wanted to hear the reassuring sound of Malachy's lovely voice. Oh, why had she delayed having a phone put on? But then, she hadn't known she'd fall in love. Fall in love? What an earth was she thinking? It was Malachy in love with her, wasn't that the story? What would it take for her to know if she was in love, if that was to happen at all? A haze of befuddlement drifted over her.

Over the next days, she was glad that the mechanic came to fix her car. The problem was nothing major, the engine was overly cold, and the battery needed recharging. She took lots of little trips into the village. The trips were an excuse to get out of the house, and to escape the utter and total emptiness she felt without Malachy's presence. At last, she smiled at people, and they smiled back. The other reason was that she was hoping to see Malachy.

They would make it seem like an innocent meeting, they could smile, and perhaps have a coffee together. It wouldn't be a lot, but it would be better than nothing. But it didn't happen. There was never a priest to be seen. She started to do crazy things. On her return home, she drove past his house, slowing as she drew near. Sometimes his car was there, other times it wasn't, other times, someone else's car was parked there. She did not go in. If she saw Tim's car, she thought she might knock and go inside. That would be safe. But unfortunately, Tim's car was never there when she was.

A few times the thought crossed her mind that she'd go to church to see him. Almost everyone else in the village went every Sunday. She didn't want them to think that she was a heathen. Going to church in these rural areas was an Irish cultural tradition, as well as a religious one. They often rolled straight from church to the pub. She was starting to realise how culture and religion were intertwined. But knowing that she hadn't come to grips with the combination of Malachy the priest, Malachy the man, and Malachy the man who was no longer in his mind fully priest, was such a bewilderment that it wasn't worth going to church simply for a glimpse of the priest-man. Who would she be seeing?

A full week past. There was no letter. Why not? What was Malachy playing at? Why hadn't he written to her as he'd promised? But then, what right did she have to expect him to respond when she was not? The thought of writing to him first, didn't cross her mind. Then one morning it came. She didn't have to be told. Her intuition leapt for joy.

She'd heard the soft thump of the letter falling on her mat. It lay on the ground, mixed with a few brown envelopes that signalled official-dom. Slowly, hesitantly, she picked the white envelope up, held it to her bosom, and went and curled up on the sofa, where memories of his body holding her were fresh in her mind. Time and time again, she had relived the memory of the last moement she sat beside him and his tentative exploring of her longing.

She read the letter quickly, then read it again slowly, savouring every word. She broke down sobbing. Never had she read such beautiful words, words that spilled over with their affection, tenderness ripe for the plucking, expectations of a life shared together, a love so deep it could hardly be contained in one man, especially when there was no release for it, no way to demonstrate his love, other than stolen kisses. It was such a beautiful letter.

A thought crossed her mind. She was in a state of bemused disbelief that she hadn't thought of it earlier. If he couldn't ring her, she would ring him. His letter hadn't given her a date and a time to meet as she'd hoped it would. She put a coat on and raced out to the car. Driving to the most obscure phone box she could find, one well off the beaten track away from the Mrs Althorps of the world, she dialled his number.

"Malachy, Malachy, Malachy," she cried out aloud. "Where are you, my dearest? I want you, I want you, I want you." She left the phone booth and strolled up and down, looking at the sheep with their beautiful, shaggy, long wool, a curly mess, and went back to the phone. She dialled again. "Please Malachy, please be home. I want to speak to you." Again, there was no answer.

She went home in a daze. "Yes Malachy, I do miss you. Yes, Malachy, I want you." She gazed at the sea. It was a wild turbulent sight, reflecting her mood. There was a third stage to Fionnuala's please. "Do I love you, Malachy? Do I?" She screamed at the powerful waves crashing the cliffs. "Tell me, do I? Do I?"

She went to bed exhausted. There was no letter the next day, or the next. She wrote one herself, pending her words carefully, telling him how much she missed him, how she longed to be in his arms again, how she'd tried to phone him, as she wanted to meet him soon, and how she couldn't bear to go much longer without seeing him and feeling his hands on her body. Writing at a maniacal pace, her writing almost scribble in haste to have it done, she drove down to the village, ostensibly to post a letter, but hoping to see his car parked there. When she couldn't see it, she drove at whim to his house. He wasn't home, there was only a tourist car in sight. All the locals had cars she now recognised. Furtively, she slipped her letter into his letterbox box flap on the front door and sped off.

The next days dragged. No contact came of any sort. A week after the first letter, another one came. It was surprisingly brief, almost formal. Sonya couldn't understand what was happening. Why was he tormenting her like this? The letter gave a day and a time to meet on the beach. It also said that if it was raining thirty minutes before the agreed time, that she should not go down to the beach, because he didn't want her to slip.

On the agreed day, she looked in total dismay and vehement anger at the weather. Enormous drops of rain hurtled from the sky from exactly thirty minutes before their agreed meeting. How could this happen to her? Sonya cried, gusts of warm torrents slid down her face, wetting the top of her jumper. Decidedly headstrong, she raced out in the fierce rain and jumped into the car. Malachy would be home. She would ring him. He was not home. "Malachy, my darling, where are you?" she screamed out aloud, her words lost to the wind.

She was not one for the strong drink, but this night, she sat staring into her fire with a large brandy balloon nursed in her hands. Trying to decipher the unbelievable bad luck she was having in not being able to contact her beloved, was driving her crazy. Her beloved? Had that phrase gone through her head? Does this mean that she does love him? What would it take for her to know that she loved him? Maybe that was it. Maybe that was the strategy Malachy was playing out. He was driving her crazy purposely so that she could admit that she did love him. No, Malachy wasn't cruel, he'd never torment her. Then what was happening?

A sudden knock at the door startled her. She stumbled to the door. "Tim," she cried, genuinely delighted to see him, "please come in."

"Sonya, what's wrong? You looked distracted to the ends of the world."

"I am Tim, have you seen Malachy? Tell me he is fine."

"He's not. He's sick."

"Sick? "Sonya's eyes widened the size of saucers. "No, no, tell me it's not too serious."

"Depends on how you look at it."

"Tim, don't tease me, what do you mean? How is he sick?"

"Love-sick, Sonya."

With this, Sonya hit him playfully, and buried her head on the sofa, close to Tim and cried.

"Talk to me, Sonya."

"How is Malachy, Tim? Please tell me in all seriousness."

"This seems serious to you."

"It is." There was a new indescribable look on her face.

"As I said, he's lovesick. He sent me over to ask you why you haven't taken the initiative to contact him."

Sonya's mouth was gaping. "I don't believe it. Do you have any idea how hard I've tried to contact him?" Sonya recounted her stories to Tim. She could see that he was reassured by them. Having seen his good friend go through private torture, he didn't want to see him hurt at the end of it.

"Sonya, he told me to tell you that he'd have the same arrangement about the beach tomorrow if that's possible. He thought of a crazy plan that might work. He's worked out that from your place you can just see the tip of the oak tree where you stopped that memorable day of your accident. If he is going down to the beach, he'll raise a red flag in it. He's got a red dishcloth he'll use."

They laughed at the cleverness of it all. "Pray that it won't rain."

"God ain't a magician Sonya, this is Ireland, it rains, sometimes forever." They laughed again. Tim's face became very serious. "Do you love the man, Sonya?"

"What do you think?" she asked, a broad smile on her face.

"I think the sooner you admit it yourself and tell him the better." He left and she felt encouraged and uplifted by his visit. She couldn't wait for tomorrow. Whatever Tim said, she would pray that it didn't rain.

The next day was cold, freezing cold, and in response to her optimism, there was no rain. She rugged up, went outside, and sure enough, the red flag could just be seen in the distance. So great was her excitement, that she nearly fell down the stairs. The wind howled as she clung onto the rail.

On the beach, she walked with hope in her step. There, walking toward her, was Malachy, he wasn't racing to her with arms outstretched to greet her like she desperately wanted. Her desire to be held was an ache.

"Malachy, run to me," she cried to the wind. "Come to me Malachy, come." But he was walking slower than normal. Something was wrong. Then, as she neared the next corner, she saw why. It took every bit of strength in her not to break down and lie in the wet sand and kick her feet like a baby throwing a tantrum.

Could life be this unfair? There on the beach, out for a marine biology excursion, was a teacher with the local school children. Malachy patiently stopped to speak with them as Sonya slowed her pace, not having it in her to be friendly to them today. She paused and sat on a rock that was sheltered away from their eyes. Waiting had never seemed so arduous.

"Sonya." Malachy didn't give her a moment to say anything. He grasped her coat to him, and his lips were hungry, finding her starving mouth. Snuggled in the folds of her coat, he found the shape of her breasts, and frantically thrust his hands over her jumper. With unexpected delight, he discovered that she was bra-less. The palms of his hands circled her aroused nipples. Her body was pressed into his, rocking against his hardness, an unabashed, wanton woman. Her head was thrown back in total pleasure. Then, as he heard young chatting voices coming closer, he moved away, saying, "come on, we have to walk a little further around the corner."

"Oh Malachy, I can't believe this. I wanted to see you so desperately. I've missed you unbearably. There's nowhere else to hide, I know every nook and cranny on this beach. I can't even hold your hand." She was whimpering. "I want you to touch me."

"Oh Sonya, such pleasures of your body are indescribable."

"Malachy, I desire you."

"Sonya my darling, I want you too, but not yet. I can't survive without you. Bother the school children. We must move away." The noise of their approach returned. "If it wasn't for Tim helping me through the countdown, I don't know how I would handle it. Ten days to go now Sonya, just ten days, and I become a free man."

In shock, they found themselves surrounded by the school children who'd seen them walking chastely together. They came racing up. Behind their backs, she whispered, "I can't cope with my disappointment. I'm going home. When can I see you again?"

They quickly made a time when they could pretend to accidentally meet in the coffee shop. With a wistful look over her shoulder, Sonya returned carefully up the steep stairs to her artist's retreat. She'd looked forward to seeing Malachy's gorgeous face again, had adored the taste of his kisses, and had forgotten how wonderful it is for a man to touch her body. Then, to have it all interrupted so quickly, was almost more than she could cope with.

Could she admit to being in love?

Twenty-One

All Sonya could think of over the next few days was meeting Malachy in the coffee shop. She put on old jeans with a figure flattering mohair sweater. Sitting by the window, reading the newspaper, she hoped that no one else would join her. For once, luck was on her side. She heard the voice she loved dearly. "Oh, hello Sonya, how nice to see you, may I join you?"

Very politely she responded, "please do."

It was a pleasant but awkward time. Everywhere Malachy went, people came up to chat to him. Sonya felt tongue-tied, unable to chat casually when she wanted to talk intimately. There was one question she wanted urgently to ask Malachy. For days, she'd thought of little else. She had remembered one occasion where she had taunted him for never having known love before, and he'd replied something to the effect that she shouldn't be sure of this.

Wanting clarification, she tentatively asked, "Malachy, have you ever loved another woman?"

"Sonya, you know I've not been able to do that."

"But have you?"

More interruptions occurred, people wanting to wish Father O'Sullivan best wishes, ask after Fionnuala, telling him the latest news about their sick mother, being friendly in a way villagers do. Sonya looked away, her frustration obvious to him alone.

"Where were we?"

She whispered, "have you loved another woman?"

"Why do you ask this?" He looked a little annoyed.

"Because I have to know."

A young mother, two children at her side, came over to tell Father O'Sullivan that her boyfriend had left her, and she didn't know how she was to manage. He gave some quick advice and arranged to drop in and see her tomorrow.

"Why do you have to know?"

"Get real Malachy, it's not an unreasonable question. I've told you about my love life."

This wasn't a good place to be having this conversation; they were having to whisper without seeming to be furtive. "I've never had a love life, Sonya."

A young man came in, fighting his tears, telling Malachy that he had received his seventy seventh job application rejection. He left dejected, despite the words of encouragement to keep trying.

"Malachy, you once told me in a passing comment that I shouldn't assume that you'd not known love." Malachy was quiet. "Quick, tell me before anyone else interrupts us."

It was too late, people came across to him, the coffee shop was filling up. It was impossible to talk privately without being overheard. Malachy knew that this attempt to snatch time together wasn't working, but he was grateful for a short time together. They left.

Furtively, Malachy said, "ring me on Thursday, at eight o'clock, I'll fill you in then."

"But Malachy, that's days away."

"That's the best I can do. I'm not going to talk openly in public."

"I don't understand," and with that, they separated as more people came to talk to Father O'Sullivan.

Life stopped still for Sonya. She went through the motions of everyday life, even dabbled at some painting, but nothing seemed to matter except for Thursday at eight o'clock. Suspicion preoccupied her. There had to be someone else, otherwise Malachy would brush the question aside as if it was meaningless. Feeling nervous, like a teenager on her first date, she rang the number.

Fury filled her when there was no answer. Malachy was playing with her emotions. This was his way of getting back to her. He was avoiding the truth, he didn't want to tell her about whatever other woman he had toyed with. Perhaps he'd thought she had played with his emotions for long enough. Now she'd see what it was like. Deep in her honesty, she knew that this was highly unlikely, Malachy was a good man. Revenge wasn't his style.

Back home, she made some hot soup, and noticed a note on her mat. She must've tripped over it when she came in the dark. It was a simple note. It read, "Dearest darling Sonya, sometimes life is cruel. How I wanted to tell you about my love for you when I knew you were to phone me tonight. I was called to little Johnny McCuskey who fell off his bike, and tragically was hit by a car. With his dying breath, he was calling for me, I'm sure you can appreciate why I had to go. Tim will take the funeral. Also, I had a call from the seminary to say that Father Paddy Ryan is seriously unwell. I'm going back to the seminary to spend the last days of leave with him. Don't despair, my darling. On Friday week, my first day as a free man, I will come to your house for dinner at seven o'clock. Until then, call Tim if you need anything. I love you, and long for the day you return my love, I remain, yours, Malachy O'Sullivan."

Never had time crawled as slowly. She tried to make herself busy by cooking, shopping, cleaning, and painting. It was almost time for another exhibition she thought. It'll help the bank balance. What she did have a lot of time for were her thoughts. Fionnuala had sent her two postcards. They were inside envelopes so that no sneaky post office person could read her messages. They had arrived on the same day, and both reminded her of her plea not to resist Malachy. Was she still resisting him? There was little resistance left in her.

A letter came from Malachy. This was handwritten, sent from the seminary. It explained to her the end of the story they had started in the coffee shop. It was meant to allay her fears. It told of a time when he had a few months of study in Rome. Every afternoon, he went to the same cafe to read the newspaper and to drink countless cups of espresso coffee. A woman came at the same time, every afternoon, and they developed a friendship. They talked mainly of intellectual matters, world politics, and the big human and theological questions of life like meaning, suffering, love, death, God, and intimacy.

He was dressed in ordinary clothes and never told her his occupation. There seemed something mysterious about her, but he didn't think to ask about the meaning of her secretiveness. They talked intensely and vigorously, and he revelled in her companionship and deep intelligence. She was a sensational, sultry woman, full of passionate intensity.

In reading this story, Sonya was feeling uncomfortably jealous. Shock flooded her as she went on to read the last page. Malachy had written that one day, the woman who was called Benita had not come in. He was surprised. He had expected her and knew precisely what intellectual issue he wanted to discuss. He opened his newspaper to see the leading story of the day. It told of the murder of Benita, a high-class call-girl.

In Malachy's letter, he told Sonya of his shock, of his intense sadness, and that curiously, there was no disgust in him when he discovered her occupation. She was the most beautiful, intelligent, lively woman friend he had ever known up until that point, outside of his sister. He had a lot to be thankful for, in having known the pleasure of her friendship. He bought flowers, paid his respects, and attended her funeral.

His last lines of the letter read, "if that's love, then I've had a taste of it. We never kissed on the lips, she would kiss me European style, one cheek then the other, on greeting me and on leaving me. We would then simply drink coffee and discuss spiritual matters as well as international politics. There was never a dull second in conversation. I loved being with her. Our debates were fascinating. Rome was never the same after her death. I haven't told anyone this story, not even Fionnuala or Tim. She is gone. I love you as ever, Malachy."

The letter left Sonya reeling. This was the stuff of best-selling novels and movies. Jealousy remained for a while, but she knew that she was being ridiculous. Malachy was a stylish, gorgeous man who was an intellectual, as well as being an entertaining conversationalist. Benita and he had enjoyed an intellectual affair, and she could cope with that, she had had many sexual relationships. She was glad she knew his story.

Her thoughts focused on Malachy's return. She prepared for the Friday night dinner meticulously. She cooked a tomato and a crab soup, baked hot rolls, bought a fine piece of duck breast and marinated it with cherries and brandy. She prepared honeyed carrots, fresh peas and broccoli, and baked a lemon cheesecake. Dermot had managed to procure her favourite bottle of Californian claret.

Deciding on what she should wear was a conundrum. It had to be seductive, but not as provocative as the dress she'd been stuck in with Tim and Malachy that fateful day that seemed so long ago. She chose a classic pale pink short dress with a low neckline. She wore lace panties and stay up lace stockings. She left her hair totally free as nature intended it, loose and beautiful.

The candles were lit, and she stood back exuberantly. This would be a marvellous night, a night to be remembered. A knock on the door came at seven o'clock promptly as she was expecting it. Her heart was racing. Malachy walked in, but curiously, did not kiss her. He held her hand and led her over to the dining room table, capturing the elusive play of the candlelight. "My darling Sonya, you look beautiful."

"Malachy, it's lovely to see you." They were almost formal with each other, unwittingly playing a clever form of foreplay.

"How lovely everything looks. Did you miss me?"

She knew from the tone of his voice that he demanded a clear answer. "Yes, I missed you. I can't live without you."

"I love you, Sonya. I have left the priesthood, not for you, but for me. Now I have left, I am free to ask you, will you marry me?"

Sonya gazed into those beautiful eyes that she had admitted she adored, looked into the shimmering candlelight, and looked back into his eyes. With a hushed voice, she said, "yes, Malachy."

"Pardon, Sonya?" Malachy looked startled.

"I love you, Malachy."

His face shone. "Oh Sonya, will you marry me?" he repeated.

"Yes Malachy, I just told you that I will. I had to wait until you left to know that you were doing it for yourself, not because of me. But yes, with your absence, I've grown to know that my life is empty without you. I love you and want to be your wife."

Malachy took hold of her hand. "You've taken off your wedding ring."

"Yes," she answered quietly. "I did that when I took Malcolm's photo off the wall the last time you were here."

"Try this, my lovely one," and from his jacket pocket, Malachy pulled out a blue velvet box.

Sonya stroked the velvet, the sensual touch making her shiver in delightful expectation. She hadn't expected anything like this. She opened the box slowly, savouring every precious second of the occasion. Inside, she saw an astonishing gold engagement ring with a large oval shaped diamond which was encircled with six deep blue sapphires. Malachy took the ring out of its box and slipped it onto Sonya's finger. It was a perfect fit. It was as if it had been designed especially for her finger.

"Oh, it is so beautiful. I love it. How did you know my size?"

"When you were dangerously ill, lying in Fionnuala's bed, I slipped your wedding ring off and drew around it on a piece of paper. I've carried the piece of paper in my wallet ever since. It was like a token, a talisman. I knew on day three of my leave that I was falling in love with you Sonya, and that I wanted to marry you, and that one day I wanted to buy you a ring like this."

"Malachy, it's such a beautiful ring. I adore it, and I love you, and I am excited about our lives together. There will be so much to talk about."

Their bodies found each other at last, and cleaved to each other hungrily, lustful, and overwhelmingly desirous. Their lips clung, while their hands found new body parts to explore. Malachy kept his fingers on top of the lace on her stockings, an iron will stopping him from going further. Her hand gripped his thigh and moved easily to feel his male firmness. He pulled away.

"I'm no longer a priest, but I am going to marry you as a virgin, my lovely one. This may sound a bit old-fashioned, but I have come this far, and that's how I want it."

"Then marry me tomorrow, Malachy, because I can't hold out for you much longer."

"There's no need for a long delay, the sooner everyone gets used to the idea of it the better."

"Tim can marry us next week," Sonya laughed, a woman in love, a woman admitting to herself and to the whole world that she was a woman in love. "How soon can we bring Fionnuala back for the wedding she joked about?"

"She's on the way home, my lovely one." They laughed their pleasure. "My forbidden love is no more, come to me my precious one, I'm going to sing you my song, and then I can smell this beautiful food." With that, he pulled Sonya onto his lap and sang her his love song.

"Malachy, I've one last question before I finally agree to marry you." For a moment, he looked concerned. "Did you really undress me without seeing my naked body?"

He laughed, relieved at the question. "I really did, my love. I was a priest then. I'm not anymore. I hoped that it was only a matter of time before you returned my love."

He pulled her body to him in eager, lustful exploration.